A Circle Is a Balloon
and Compass Both

STORIES ABOUT HUMAN LOVE

Ben Greenman

A Circle Is a Balloon
and Compass Both

STORIES ABOUT HUMAN LOVE

Ben Greenman

MACADAM CAGE

MacAdam Cage
155 Sansome Street, Suite 550
San Francisco, CA 94104
www.MacAdamCage.com

Library of Congress Cataloging-in-Publication Data
Greenman, Ben.
A circle is a balloon and compass both :
stories about human love / by Ben Greenman.
p. cm.
ISBN 978-1-59692-207-5 (alk. paper)
I. Title.
PS3607.R463C57 2007
813'.6—dc22
2006103280

Paperback edition: April, 2007
ISBN 978-1-59692-230-3

Some of these stories first appeared in the following publications,
often in a slightly different form:
"Black, Gray, Green, Red, Blue" on *McSweeneys.net*, "How Little We Know
About Cast Polymers, And About Life" in *Stumbling and Raging*
(MacAdam/Cage 2005), "The Re-Education of M. Grooms" in *Opium*,
"My Decorous Pornography" on *Nerve.com*, "Batting Cleanup" in *Elysian
Fields Quarterly*, "The Duck Knows How to Make the Most of Things" in
The L Magazine, and "In the Air Room" in *Zoetrope: All Story*.
Book and cover design by Dorothy Carico Smith

To Gail

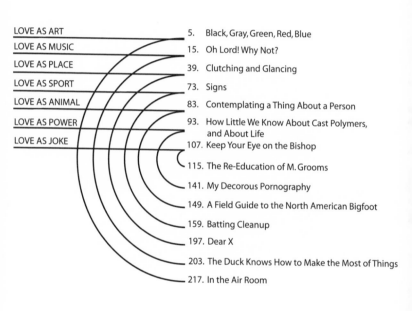

Introduction

I was Ben's second-grade art teacher. I tried at the time to get him to see that the world was composed of both large movements and small decisions. Did he grasp it? Not at the time—mostly he just drew trees with odd-shaped fruit hanging from them—but he appears to have made up ground since then. I especially appreciate the way that the title of the book holds together the opposites of orientation (the compass) and escape (the balloon), not to mention the way the title conflates the zero of nullity and the O of orgasm. Has anyone ever titled a book with the shape of a circle before? I do not know but I hope it happens again and again.

That is all I have to say, and still I have something more to say. Years later, I encountered Ben again. By then I was not teaching art full-time, but substituting in that same school district, and Ben was not a second grader, but a tenth grader. Eight years had passed in my life; it was as if eight hundred had passed in his. Substitutes are the strangest kind of monarch, complicit in their own overthrow, and I decided that day to give the children an impossible assignment. "In your life, you will have to choose between options," I said. "Write a short story that justifies not one choice or another, but the process of choosing." I made the assignment from fun, perhaps even a touch of sadism. I could not have expected that the students would rise to the challenge. Many of them did a superb job with such an abstract assignment. Something about Ben's response struck a chord in me, and I kept it among my papers. When I learned he was working on a story collection, I sent it to him, and he called me, laughing. "You know why I wrote that?" he said. "To impress a girl. A specific girl. She was sitting to the right of me. Her name was Mary Pollock." I laughed, too, even though I think that he was not being honest. He did not write it to impress a girl so much as to calm himself in the presence of a girl he wished to impress. This is why we create: to keep our demons down without banishing them entirely.

Enough speculation. I give you his piece, revived (and revised) after a span of twenty years:

Life was a platform, and he had everything he needed there: a phone, food, companionship. He was happy. Then he looked to his right and saw a platform that was slightly higher, maybe three feet or so. He thought to himself that he might be happier on the other platform. The second platform also had a telephone, food, a companion. But he felt certain that the telephone was of a superior design and color, that the food was prepared better, that the companion would entertain and enrich him in ways that his companion could not. After all, the other platform was higher. He was consumed by the thought of jumping to it. He wasn't sure if he could make the jump. He needed to make the jump. He agonized over it. He lost sleep, and when he did sleep, he dreamed about the slightly higher platform. Then one day he woke with the courage to jump. He knew that it was the day. He placed a final call on the telephone on the platform. He ate a final meal. He told his companion that he would be only one platform away, and that since it was higher, he would be able to jump back whenever he wanted. Then he took a running start and jumped, pushing off as powerfully as he could, certain that he would need all his effort to reach the higher platform. In the air he worried about falling into the void between platforms. What would that be? Death? Solitude? Neither was a thought that comforted him. Somehow, miraculously, his foot found the edge of the other platform. He landed there in a heap. He looked around. The phone looked about the same. The food looked about the same. The companion looked about the same. But at least he was higher. Then, as he was commending himself for having the courage to jump, the platform started to sink down, imperceptibly at first but then enough that he could see it move. It came to him in a flash: he had forgotten to figure in the effect of his own weight. He looked across at his former platform and it was rising. He closed his eyes. He opened them. He was standing on a platform. He had everything he needed there: a phone, food, companionship. Then he looked to his right and he saw a platform that was slightly higher, maybe three feet or so.

— Marie Palermo, 2005

In every thing there are two things. We can choose one sometimes and the other at other times. In this way, we can imagine that we are making choices when in fact we are doing anything but choosing.

—*Arturo Respero*

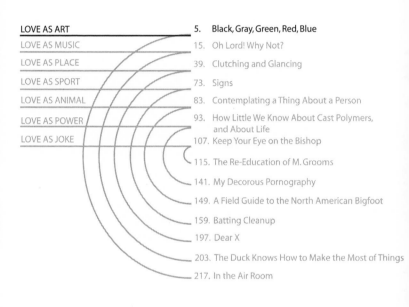

Black, Gray, Green, Red, Blue:
A Letter From a Famous Painter on the Moon

Dear Lucille Bogan,

Fifteen years ago, when I left the Earth, I was just another struggling painter in New York City. My canvases were of two varieties: expressionistic black-and-gray cityscapes that often featured hunched figures collapsed inside oversized trench coats, and brightly colored nudes of you. One June day, I made up my mind to abandon the darker side of my nature and embrace what was good in the world. I came to your apartment and leaned on the buzzer. "Hello?" you said. "It's me," I said. We had dinner. We had dessert. We went to bed and drank a few glasses of red wine, after which I made my case for embracing what was good in the world. "You know what that means? For us?" I said. You seemed to. We went to sleep perpendicular to one another. Your head was on my chest. The next morning, when I woke up, I was on the moon. You were not. I cursed. I kicked a stone and it flew for what seemed like miles. Low gravity has its advantages. By noon, though, I had recovered my composure sufficiently to invent the style of painting that would bring me international—indeed, interplanetary—renown. It was brighter and more vivid, even, than the nudes. It exploded with color. Here on the moon that kind of thing was in great demand, and has continued to be.

Dear Lucille Bogan,

Four days ago here on the moon I fell and hit my head on the corner of a table. I got up almost immediately—low gravity has its advantages—but I had a dizzy spell, then a fainting spell, then a swoon. It turns out that the culprit was not the fall at all but rather a moderately severe case of something called Longtime Moon Resident Dissociative Disorder, or Lam-rod. Symptoms include slight dizziness. I'm going to go lie down for a moment.

Dear Lucille Bogan,

Another symptom of Lam-rod is that you tend to start letters over again even though you have started them already.

Dear Lucille Bogan,

Last night I went to see a friend of mine named Krystof Janikowski. He's here on the moon, too. Has been since ninety-two. He came here with his son Krystof Janikowski Jr. Krystof Janikowski likes to call him "the Hebe dwarf" because I guess the mother is Jewish. Krystof Janikowski also likes to pretend that he hates his ex-wife, although I happen to know that they had a perfectly amicable separation and that he still treasures her opinion on most matters. Krystof Janikowski wanted to discuss a book he has written. It's called *Blocaine and Shabu*, and it's a blaxploitation thriller set on the Earth in which one guy does another guy a solid. Krystof Janikowski is a god-damned idiot, and I told him so, right in front of that Hebe dwarf. He took a swing at me, and landed a punch on my shoulder, but it barely hurt. Low gravity has its advantages.

Dear Lucille Bogan,

Another effect of Lam-rod is that you start to question yourself. This letter seems no more interesting to me than a Fabian milk report. And maybe *Blocaine and Shabu* isn't that bad after all.

Dear Lucille Bogan,

Or is it terrible? This Lam-rod is immensely frustrating. I am a famous artist. My work has been exhibited in the Art Museum of the Moon, the Modern

Moon Art Museum, and the Lunar Art Institute. So why can't I render a confident and irrevocable judgment on the quality of *Blocaine and Shabu*? I am going to the doctor right now.

Dear Lucille Bogan,
The doctor, who was short and who would have been considered fat back when I was on Earth but is now simply round—low gravity has its advantages—gave me a green pill. Doctors here on the moon are like that. They think that pills solve everything. When I was walking back from the doctor's office, I saw Krystof Janikowski. He turned to avoid me, but I went up to him and clapped him on the back. "You know," I said, "my opinion about the book is simply my opinion. If I had listened to every jerk who expressed skepticism during the three hours it took me to become a famous painter, I might have never done so." Krystof Janikowski laughed. "I know," he said. "But I appreciate your honesty. And I think I figured out the problem: I think the title should be reversed. *Shabu and Blocaine* is much better." I shrugged. It didn't seem to matter. So maybe the doctor and his green pill were the answer after all.

Dear Lucille Bogan,
Now it is tomorrow, and I am in such despair that I must call the doctor again.

Dear Lucille Bogan,

The doctor told me that despair is a side effect of the green pill. "First you feel real good," he said, "and then you feel real bad." I asked him why he didn't warn me about that before. "Because I am better friends with Krystof Janikowski," he said. "The Hebe dwarf is my godson." He laughed merrily. "You'll want to tear off your face all afternoon," he said, "but it should be gone by tomorrow."

Dear Lucille Bogan,

Now it is tomorrow again and I am in even greater despair. I called the doctor. "Crap," he said, and he rushed right over. He gave me a red pill and then began to take my pulse, to listen to my breathing, to palpate me about the neck and jaw. Then he stopped. "Whose paintings are these?" he said. I told him they were mine. "They are beautiful," he said. "Absolutely beautiful." I told him that I was famous. "I don't really follow the art world," he said. "But I know what I like. I especially like that one." I followed his finger and found that he was pointing toward a small canvas near the bookshelf. It was a foot square, hung at diamond angle. It was painted from memory. It was a portrait of you. At once, my despair lifted. Unfortunately, it was replaced by a crippling pain that radiated from my Adam's apple and quickly reached my head and my stomach. I fell to the ground, screaming. "Aha," the doctor said. "I think I know what the matter is." He produced a blue pill and threw it into the air. While it fell, he explained to me what he thought was happening; low gravity has its advantages. "The red pill," he said, "tends to dredge up emotional pain and then, when the source of that pain is identified, convert all psychological burden into acute physical pain." I asked him what the blue pill did. "Painkiller," he said, and left.

Dear Lucille Bogan,

Another effect of Lam-rod is that you tend to digress before you get to the point. Luckily, the red pill curbs that digressive effect somewhat. So this is the point: I miss you. I miss you terribly. I miss you horribly. I miss you painfully. I know that I am expressing myself clumsily. I am a painter, not a writer. I regret almost every second that has passed since I went to sleep on the Earth and woke up on the moon. I was blithely unaware of how wretched and empty my life would feel without you. Remember? I cursed and kicked a stone. These are the behaviors of a child who has misplaced a toy, not a man who has been separated from a woman. Once, about a year ago, I was walking outside, and I saw Krystof Janikowski with Krystof Janikowski Jr. This was when *Blocaine and Shabu* was just a glint in his eye; he talked about it, but he had not written a word. Krystof Janikowski was on his back on a blanket on the ground. He had his hands behind his head. He was sunbathing and listening to the radio. Krystof Janikowski Jr. was running around, playing, making noise. Boys will be boys. But then that little Krystof Janikowski Jr. came and lay down on the blanket. He tucked himself into the crook of his arm, and then he shifted so that he was perpendicular to his father. That little Hebe dwarf looked like he was in heaven. I started to cry. At the time, I had no idea why.

Dear Lucille Bogan,

This blue pill is making a fool of me. It does nothing. The pain is still in my throat and head and belly. I long for the days before the red pill, for the days when I was afflicted only with Lam-rod. And the despair has returned with even greater ferocity. Evidently the green pill works in cycles. This morning I dashed off a small painting, in dour black and gray, of a lone figure scuttling across a rainy alleyway. When I finished, I had a sudden urge to climb to the roof of my house and jump off. I didn't, though, because I would probably just float to the ground like a feather. Low gravity has its disadvantages.

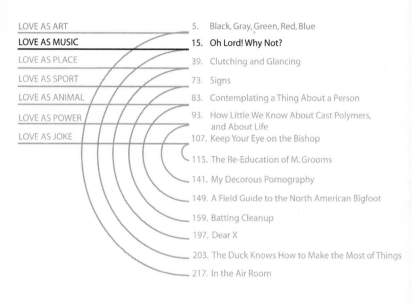

Oh Lord! Why Not?

1.

I am a pop singer. So are you. That's the deal these days. Everyone is. The air is filled with music. Our ears—our collective ears—have never been so regularly served. Music comes through the radio, through the television, through the computer, through the phone, and through small electronic cards inserted into the daily newspaper. At the present moment, I am listening simultaneously to three songs that were written and performed in the last week by people who live within a four-hundred-yard radius of my house. There is "Find the Cost of Love" by Anton Ellsberg (older gentleman who lives around the corner, not particularly friendly), "Saying Her Name" by Peter Scopitus (handsome young guy who recently bought the house across the street, probably gay), and "Yeah!

Yeah! Yeah! (There's a Frog in My Pool)" by Lee-Lee Parker (assistant manager at my Chestnut Avenue restaurant, wears invisible braces). Everyone and their mother is a pop singer. I mean this just as it is said—Antonia Parker, Lee-Lee's mother, has just released a song called "Come on Now Inside and Warm Me Up." I haven't heard it yet, but I am told that the melody isn't half bad. Lee-Lee provides backup vocals, which she practices at the restaurant. "Inside, inside," she sings softly as she stands over the grill, "Me up, me up."

2.

I am not a pop singer. Rather, I am more than one. I am a pop star, or was. As a young man of eighteen, I wrote and recorded a song about love and friendship called "Strength in Numbers" (#4 Pop). It was followed by a series of other hits: "I'm Not Going to Say That to You" (#11 Pop), "Mission Bell" (#6 Pop), "I Cried Your Eyes Out" (#12 Pop), "Losers Weepers" (#7 Pop), and "The King Cobra" (#2 Pop). "The King Cobra" was a rock-and-roll song, but it inspired a popular dance of the same name. You put your hands on either side of your neck and then turn them rapidly outward in the fashion of a hood, then you extend two fingers on your right hand and hold them in front of your mouth like a forked tongue. Now you're doing the King Cobra. It was the lead single from an album grandiosely named *Ophiophagy*, which was a word I had just learned and of which I was possibly too proud. Other songs on the album included "Jacobson's Organ" (#88 Pop) and "Oh Lord! Why Not?" (did not chart). When we filmed the video, I wanted to use real snakes, but the director insisted on hiring a dozen young models and having them dress in snake costumes. In retrospect, this instinct was sound. This is the advice I give to all young people, including my own son: listen to others. Sometimes you are blinded by the need to advance yourself, whereas they are not. They may be blinded by the need to advance themselves, but it is up to you to see their wisdom through the fog of self-interest. My son listens to me intently when I am giving this advice, which suggests that he may not need it. He is seven years old and a beautiful child for many reasons, not the least of which is that he is in no hurry to record a pop song. "I figure I'll do it when I have something to say," he said. Love of my life. I took him bowling and then out for ice cream—the good kind, not the soft-serve we have at Burger Man—to reward him.

3.

"The King Cobra," which was kept from the top of the charts by a ballad called "Please Don't Plead," was my last major hit. As a result, it is the song with which I am most strongly associated. Many items that I own, including my car, my favorite Zippo, and a large number of white leather jackets, have a cobra logo or insignia. The song was even featured in a series of action films starring a man named Jake Patko, whose nickname was "The Snake." Thanks principally to "The King Cobra," I made some money, though not as much as I would have made if my business manager had been honest, and I used it to buy a pair of Burger Man franchises. Those were the cornerstones of my empire, and in each of those two original stores, I hung gold-record certificates of my most famous songs. The King Cobra even got a sandwich named after it: chicken with hot sauce, because "it has bite." When I stopped being a pop singer, it bruised my ego more than I would have expected. I used to wake up in the middle of the night and sit in the living room with a guitar, trying to write something else catchy and meaningful. All that came to me was nonsense, doggerel or worse. The emotional effects lingered. My wife, Gloria, who had met me when I was famous— she was one of the dancers on the "King Cobra" video—was not entirely pleased to find herself suddenly married to a Burger Man franchisee, and we had some tough times that involved a period of separation and the shattering of car windows with golf clubs. Then came therapy, which did wonders. I spent seven weeks in a little office with a large woman with small glasses and emerged a more balanced man. Trivial things once set me off—the headline news, the weather. For me, they are usually one in the same. We live in the narrow seam between two temperate zones and, as a result, consistently experience extreme weather: big, thick snowflakes that the news anchors call "snowcakes," hot drops of rain. Thanks to therapy, I reached a point where the weather meant no more to me than…well, than weather. I learned to wake up, kiss my wife, hug my son, and drive to work, humming all the way. But then came this new era, in which everyone and their mother is a pop singer. Now that's unpleasant weather. You'd think that the explosion of pop singers would make it easier for me to get back in the game, but the fact is that there is no more game. To tell you how we came to this sad circumstance—as a nation, as a culture—I will need to take a drink. I have already filled the shot glass, which is decorated with a decal of a king cobra, with whiskey. "Ready for venom," I say to no one in particular, and I kill the shot.

4.

I once knew a man who said, "History happens slowly." He was a homeless man, probably retarded, who liked to dumpster-dive behind my flagship Burger Man restaurant, weather permitting, and I didn't put much stock in his proclamations. In fact, I have found that often history happens with blazing speed. Take the Era of the Pop Singer. We were like any other culture. We had our businessmen and our teachers and our doctors and our priests and our pop singers. Each profession respected the integrity of the other professions. When I was traveling by airplane, I would often sit next to a lawyer or a marketing manager. I would enter into conversation with him or her, express an interest (rarely feigned) in his or her career, and then field questions about my own career. "Choruses are usually written first," I'd say, "and then verses." Or: "I'm not sure how I came up with 'Hear the sound of the mission bell / At the bottom of a wishing well.' Sometimes I think those things are given to me by a divine intelligence." The comments I made were not markedly different from those I made on late-night talk shows or between songs onstage, but they were received with more than simple curiosity. They were part of a dialogue. Then, over the course of a few months, everything shifted. Change had been lurking and it struck. A company in San Jose released a piece of free software that made it easier than ever to construct a song in the privacy of your own home. A large company in Boston refined its online distribution model. And suddenly, voilà!, everyone was a pop singer. I cannot stress how rapid the change was. One day, there were only a few pop singers, men and women who had enjoyed brief periods of national renown and then suffered through long stretches of diminishing returns—mall tours, oldies packages, occasional appearances on television sitcoms where we were, by mere fact of our existence, the butt of jokes. We were a brotherhood of sorts.

When I would see the others—once I saw Rick Hayward in a hotel, and once I sat next to Kayla Jay on a plane—we would hardly speak. Anything we had to say to one another was already alive within us. Then the next minute, we were nothing special. There were as many pop songs as there were people. This cultural revolution brought about the Litt Act, which was a bill sponsored by the junior senator from California. By the terms of the Litt Act, each and every American is permitted to release only one pop song. It rises as high as it rises, then it falls away, and people go back to their lives. If a person was a pop singer (or star) before the Era of the Pop Singer, he or she is not allowed to release any songs at all. The Litt Act was denounced by civil libertarians, but it passed, and now it is law. Senator Litt himself recorded a song to commemorate the passage of the legislation: "Follow the Rules Behind Me," which seemed by its title to suggest that Litt expected it to hit the top ten, at least, but in fact it barely made the top fifty. This is what I mean when I say that there is no more game. We have a nation of pop singers, but no pop stars.

5.
There are millions of examples of this new phenomenon: as many examples as there are Americans, as I have said. I will give you one. Three years ago, my next-door neighbor was your basic run-of-the-mill

thirtysomething lawyer, James Entiendo, who lived a
perfectly respectable life with his wife, Lily. He and I
would see each other over the fence in our backyard
during cookouts and other summer-type activities.
His daughter was a few years older than my son; they
were friendly but not friends; once the four of us went
to the circus together. The closest I ever got to James
Entiendo, in any actual sense, was about a year ago, at
a cocktail party, when Lily got more drunk than any of
us could have anticipated and asked Gloria if we had
ever considered swinging. Gloria, who was equally
drunk, told Lily that she had considered it, that the two
of us had in fact talked about it—you know how it is,
your body gets older, your mind stays young, you
grasp for a way of maintaining your vitality. I think the
two of them made out on the patio, but the next
morning, when the alcohol had drained away, they
were both mortified, and the subject was never again
raised. I am fairly certain that I would not have gone
through with it. I love my wife, somewhat desperately,
so much so that I will rarely speak of her. What parts
of her I can address directly I route through my son,
who I can love because he is himself and also because
he is of her. I have said that my wife was not entirely
pleased to find herself married to a Burger Man franchisee. That is not exactly true. The truth is that she
was entirely not pleased. While I was a pop star, she
told me daily, and often breathlessly, that she loved me

more than the stars, moon, and sun. Now that I am not a pop star, she says that she respects and admires me for recognizing that I had to trade in stardom for an existence as a more stable provider. "I respect and admire you," she says, clipping the words. More to the point: she believes what she says, but she sleeps on her half of the bed, rarely crossing over, and she is more and more indifferent to the monthly romantic dinner that we used to depend upon like the needful thumping of our own hearts. At that same party where the women discussed swinging, James and I talked about my career as a pop star, and James, who was slightly drunk, said that he had an idea for a song. "Yeah," I said. "People always have those kinds of ideas." I was sober and a little surly. I had just bought four more Burger Man restaurants, but Gloria was not the only one bothered by the curve of the road, as you might say. James laughed. "I'm sure you get that all the time," he said. "Let's talk about something less annoying." We talked about the damage to his garage roof, which wasn't less annoying. The conversation about his pop-singer aspirations was forgotten. When the Era of the Pop Singer began, I dreaded running into James. I knew what he would tell me. A bad rain one day trapped us underneath a local oak tree. "I did a song," he said. He was modest enough about it—he only hummed me a little snippet, and then reddened and shook his head—but I knew he was on to something. What I didn't know is how on he was. The song was "Seek America" (#2 Pop). You know it. Of course you do. It was the hit of the summer: "Seek America / America's the goal / Seek America / Inside your American soul." As it was headed up the charts, I found myself falling victim to all manner of minor physical ailments. I had a headache, a toothache, constipation, sinus trouble. I gobbled aspirin, tipped bottles of cough syrup down my throat, consumed a garden's worth of medicinal herbs. Nothing worked. One night I got my guitar out of the closet and strummed a few chords. I guess I can admit that I was thinking of writing a song, and I had a first line that, for one merciful second, took my headache away, "All my life's been diggin' but I've still got far to go." No second line, though, and the headache came back strong. The day that James's song reached its peak position, I had a throbbing hammer-knock that settled in behind my eyes. It woke me up, prevented me from kissing Gloria and even my son, and eventually forced me to vomit into the bin at Burger Man where we keep the miniature action figures that we hand out to kids. The day was hot—temperatures had exceeded all predictions—but still I sent Lee-Lee out back to hose down the toys. "And hose yourself down if you feel a heatstroke coming on," I said. I watched her through the narrow vertical window, hosing down the bin like the employee of the month that she was, and would in my heart forever be. She set an example, you could say, and so I forced myself to make a congratulatory phone call to James. "Thank you so much," he said. "I'm sure that it's not going to go any higher than this." He was right. It turned around and tumbled down the charts the very next week. My headache cleared right up. The next time I saw James, he was on his way to an appointment with a car company that wanted to use "Seek America" in its commercials. I reminded myself that he would never chart higher than I did, but when I thought about it, that was no consolation at all.

6.

The achievements of my block were not unrepresentative. I read the papers, where it was made abundantly clear that nearly everyone was a pop singer. A woman a few neighborhoods over hit number one, and her boss gave her a ten-thousand-dollar bonus. A pair of identical twins, separated since birth, charted with extremely similar songs, delighting biologists. A man in Ohio snuck back onto the charts a second time, using a false name, and he was sentenced to a month in prison and a two-thousand-dollar fine under the terms of the Litt Act. News of pop singers had replaced news of the weather almost completely. It came in from all directions, but my block was the one that I concentrated on. Ann Weldon, the mail carrier, kicked off the month with a single called "Ooh, Ooh, You're the One for Me" (#19 Pop). Then Jack up the street weighed in with "I Got Something" (#24 Pop), and his wife, Estelle, answered with "Big Bright World" (#33 Pop). Jack and Estelle were always a cheery couple. I'm sure it didn't even bother them that they didn't go top twenty. I read the article about them to Gloria one morning over breakfast. Gloria didn't have much to say in response. She had the same problems with pop singers that I did. Her tastes, as I have said, tended more toward stardom. And while this strengthened the bond between us, it also drove us apart. I was of mixed minds regarding her restraint. I appreciated that she wasn't the kind of woman who would, like Estelle, just cook up a song and place it on the charts, but I also wanted her to record something, for the simple reason that someone I knew had to beat James Entiendo. My interest in this matter had begun with my headaches. It had sprung from the pain in my skull. Over the weeks it grew until it could fairly be called an obsession. I was convinced that a number-one hit from the neighborhood, written and performed by someone other than James Entiendo, was the only thing that would set the world right again. The songs on the block kept coming: Lucas DiLiberto's "Two Ways Back" (#28 Pop), Sadie Shaw's "Put It in the Cart" (#10 Pop), and Little Benny Arthur's "Hidden Agenda" (#15 Pop). The homeless retarded guy who hung out behind the Burger Man recorded "Preventable Famine

Candy," which started out surprisingly strong but stalled at #17. Then one day, in my office at Burger Man, I came up with an idea that was so elegantly simple that I felt stupid that it hadn't occurred to me earlier. It was like the time that I decided to sell pineapple milkshakes and call them "Tropical Winter." I was a former pop star. I had a stellar sense of popcraft. I was the only man on the block who had written the couplet "A teardrop falls from eye to ground / Over time that's what I've found." What I needed to do was to plant ideas in other people's heads, seed them with lyrics and melodies, and then watch as their songs shot up the charts—ideally, right past "Seek America." For my first test subject, I chose May Alderson, who lived two blocks over. May was in her midtwenties, pretty, with a small but effective range of appealingly sleepy expressions. She and I had flirted over the years and then, during the period of difficulty in my marriage, embarked on a brief affair. Nothing turned to love, though, and this enabled us to remain friends when Gloria and I patched things up. Once every few weeks I ran into May in the supermarket, and we had coffee at the small round tables that were set up by the bakery section. The first time I saw May after I had come up with my Tropical Winter–caliber idea, we got to talking, and I steered the conversation around to the subject of relationships. May was seeing a man who lived in California.

"Might as well be Mars," she said. "Don't knock Mars," I said. "I hear it's nice this time of year." May frowned sleepily. She had done this often during our brief affair. It was one of the most attractive things about her. "I just don't know what to do," she said. "I really want things to work out with this guy." This was my moment. I had counted on it and it had arrived as anticipated. "Well," I said, letting the word dangle as if I was thinking about what to say next, "if you can't be with the one you love, hate the one you love." You could call it a quip, but a quip would not have been written and rewritten as I sat at my desk that morning at Burger Man. May laughed. For a second, the sleepiness vanished from her eyes. It was replaced by a look I can only describe as a guarantee of achievement. The next week, there it was, her song. She had shortened up the title to "Hate the One You Love," which I thought was a little too blunt, but I had no quarrel with the material. Of all the songs generated by our neighborhood, it was the one that I thought had the most going for it. She had done me proud. The day it was released, I bought all the trade magazines for the first time since I was a pop star. "One of the most trenchant subversions of a tried-and-true pop classic in weeks." "A killer melody and a surprisingly strong vocal." "Top ten at least." I was so sure that it would do what I wanted it to do that I took my son out for ice cream again, and we stopped to bowl on the way home. "This is the most fun," he said, rolling a spare with bits of chocolate at the corner of his mouth. I didn't have any answer except to hug him. But popular tastes sometimes resist artistic excellence, and May Alderson's song only reached #16. The next time I ran into her in the supermarket, she was beaming. Her boyfriend had taken the song personally, and he had left California as a result. "It was a number-one hit in my heart," she said. I laughed and told her she should have recorded a song with that title instead: "Number-One Hit in My Heart." "I don't care about what doesn't matter," she said. "Or that one," I said, but the joke was thinning out.

7.

Another rainstorm, another day trapped under the oak tree with my neighbor and fellow pop singer James. "It's a bad storm," he said. "I hear there's a danger of flash flooding," he said. "We're built on a hill, but there's a larger hill farther uptown that would put us out of business if it keeps raining like this forever," he said. I didn't say anything. Instead I watched the fat drops of warm rain splash against his black leather shoes. Finally he left off with the weather. "I'm just having trouble with this idea," he said. "The idea that I could rise high and then fall away." I still refused to answer him, but I met his gaze so that he knew that I was with him on this one. This licensed him to buddy up to me, and he did. He told me that he had ordered crates of "Seek America" memorabilia, including a poster in which he had an eagle on each shoulder. "Real eagles," he said. "They weren't cheap." Then he told me that he had been distant from Lily, distant from his daughter, that even though a pop song was just a pop song, it had done something to him. "It feels like a conversion," he said. "As if the man I was is no longer, and this new man, newly born, does not yet know the rules." The rain had let up now, and normally this was something that James would have remarked upon, but he was past the point of noticing the weather. He was also past the point of waiting for me to answer him. "I wrote a letter of resignation at the firm," he said. "It's sitting on the far right corner of my desk while I decide what to do with it," he said. "I could never have imagined leaving the law, and now I can't bear the thought of continuing to practice," he said. The sun was baking us now. His shoes were almost dry. "Have I changed or has everything else changed, revealing my true self in the process?" he said. "This stuff just weighs on you." He was waiting for a nod from me that never came. He leaned out from under the tree, checked the weather, and went off home. That night, Gloria and I were supposed to have our monthly dinner, but instead there was a note on the kitchen counter. "Had to take the car into the shop," it said. "Rattle rattle, you know." My son and I ate homemade pizza and I let him watch a cartoon about a brother and sister who lived on the moon. Gloria came home halfway through, angry from the way the mechanic had treated her, angrier at me for breaking the no-cartoons-after-dinner rule, and went straight to the shower. Because the universe is only benign if you refuse to see it for what it is, the car commercial with "Seek America" came on the TV just as I was turning it off. I didn't hear much, only the part that went "Millions of people just like me / Stretched as far as the eye can see," but it was enough. I got my guitar out of the closet and gave it another shot. It wasn't as complete in its desolation as it usually was. Two lines this time: "I wish I was back inside that darkened place / I wish that I had never seen your face." I guess it was a love song, moody but devoted, one of those songs where the woman is a ghost in the house of the man's head and after weeks of trying unsuccessfully to get the haunt out he just lies down on the bed and dies inside the memory of her. Those two lines hung in the air like steam as I strummed the same sad chord over and over again. When Gloria came out of the bathroom, I pretended to be asleep.

8.

Gloria borrowed my car while hers was in the shop, and though I planned to take my son to a movie, the winds were up, and so we went to fly a kite in the park. "I love spending time with you," I said, and tousled his hair. Other fathers and sons were out there, flying kites with fancy shapes—dragons, fish, one massive pirate ship. I had a king cobra kite at home, but it embarrassed me, and instead I had brought a simple triangular kite decorated with a picture of a cartoon dog. We got to business: I got the kite up in the air, handed my son the reel, and he played it out or in, trying to keep the thing aloft. Every few minutes it went into irons and came crashing back to the ground, which seemed to please my son immensely. About fifteen minutes after we arrived, I noticed that James was in the park. He was wearing a bright yellow shirt that said "Seek America" in embroidered letters over the right breast. "You here with your daughter?" I said, trying to be neighborly. "No," he said. "She's at the movies with Lily, and I'm killing time until I have to pick them up." He came and stood next to us. The three of us smiled into the sun and the wind. It felt almost like friendship. Then James started telling me how to fly the cartoon dog. "Get it up above the tree-line," he said. "That way it catches enough wind to stay up." He was right, I knew, but my son was having fun running back and forth until he caught a dead patch. James and I watched as the kite shot up and then turned and headed earthward. "That must look familiar to you," I said. I was joking about "Seek America," and how it had done on the chart, but James wasn't listening. He was more concerned with high-handing me about the kite. "Make sure the bridle is in the right place," he said. "I think the way you have it, the bird comes down too fast." I didn't want to talk about the kite. I didn't want to talk about much of anything, except the things that were different, and why they had changed. "How's work?" I said. "Given any more thought to that resignation?" He laughed. "I did," he said, "and then I talked to Lily, and we went through it very carefully, went through all the ways that I'm succeeding and all the wonderful things that come to us as a result of my success. Why disrupt a perfect life?" I thought about tackling him, or punching him in the face. I think I could have broken his nose. I know for a fact that I could have split his lip, and that would have looked pretty spectacular, the firework of blood all over the front of his bright yellow shirt. Just then the kite came down between us with a thud. It saved his life—his perfect goddamn life. He said good-bye, went off to collect Lily and his daughter. My son and I walked home. I should have tousled his hair again, but my fist was clenched so tight that it felt like it was cramping.

9.

It didn't occur to me right away. I was distracted by problems at home. A few days after my son and I flew the dog kite in the park, Gloria worked up the courage to tell me she was miserable. She didn't say "divorce," but she said enough other things that I saw the word carved out in the negative space of the conversation. We agreed to wait a month and revisit the subject. I started spending all my spare time at Burger Man. Lee-Lee had her braces off, which made her so happy that she spent most afternoons gladly doing whatever dumb task needed doing, whistling "Yeah! Yeah! Yeah! (There's a Frog in My Pool)" as she went. Her mother, Antonia, came by to tell me that Lee-Lee loved her job; I thought about trying for something with Mrs. Parker, but I didn't have the heart. Most nights I brought home pints of soft-serve ice cream for my son, who regarded them with appropriate suspicion. The guitar stayed in the closet, forgotten, and forgotten is a very long time indeed. But then one night Gloria volunteered to take the couch, and I agreed in the interest of compromise, and stayed awake listening to the driving rain on the windows that had become more rule than exception. Eventually I found myself staring at the closet door. What's in there? I asked myself. I didn't know the answer. I didn't retrieve the guitar, but I did dream about music—more specifically, I dreamed a song. "The bird comes down too fast / It knows the flight can't last" was how it started, and this time it didn't end after one line, or two. It went on through a second verse, a chorus, a bridge, and a reprise. It was all there, beautifully so, and even waking up didn't cost me anything. I thought about asking Gloria to record it—as another line in the song explains, "A lovely gift / Can heal a painful rift"—but decided instead to give it to May Alderson for her boyfriend, who she assured me had a pleasant tenor voice. Besides, he was new in town, and as a result would engender less resentment from the neighbors when his song, "The Bird Comes Down Too Fast," did exactly what I knew it would do, soaring into the top ten, biding its time at number four for two weeks, and then ascending, with such confidence that it seemed like destiny, straight up to number one.

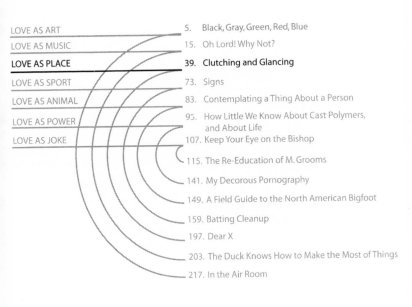

Clutching and Glancing

On the morning of January 22, a Monday, I met Arthur Manley in the lower lobby of the Grand Palms Hotel in Miami. Octagonal, and lit by an enormous skylight that capped a four-floor atrium, the lobby assumed the color of the sky, which that January 22 was also the precise hue of Arthur Manley's suit—slate gray. It hung on him quite nicely as he walked toward me. No one would have disputed its elegance. I could look straight at the man, at his broad shoulders and his long, straight legs, and pretend that I was admiring the suit. And because I could, I did. Who would blame me?

I expected that this figure, whom I did not yet know as Arthur Manley, would pass me with an approving nod, or stop to sit in one of the rattan chairs between us, or step onto the patio and light up a cigarette. I had never seen him before, and you simply don't expect a man you have never seen before to speak to you. But speak to me he did. "Hi there," he said. "Hello." Then he checked the time on a beautiful gold stem watch. He was in his late twenties, probably, not much older than I, and his straight black hair fell in uneven bangs that seemed more the product of calculated nonchalance than a bad haircut. No man with an expensive gray suit and a beautiful gold stem watch is victimized by a barber. After he spoke, he smiled, and the corners of his mouth curled upward with what seemed to be amusement, although it could have been slight cruelty. I said hello in return, and then we stood there saying nothing. We could have been statues; in some sense, we were. "Well," he said finally, "I'd like to stay and talk to you. I saw you when I was checking in. You were standing next to the big planter then, and I thought that I should talk to you. 'That's the kind of woman I need to talk to more often,' I thought. But I won't keep you from your work. And at any rate, I'm sure we'll meet again. I'm Arthur Manley. And unless you're wearing someone else's name tag, you're Deborah." Then he was off.

As he slipped away through one of the slant-corners of the lobby, I noticed that he had a slight limp. It made him lay off his left leg and gave him a rolling gait that was, in its own way, as seductive as his smile. I straightened the dried flowers on the table, made sure the bottlebrushes and the bougainvillea looked right, and then began to empty the ashtrays, for that was my job that winter.

A few days later, I was out on the patio, smoking cigarettes on my break and talking to Elsie, another girl who was taking time to clarify her muddy life. Elsie was tall and blond, with slightly collapsed features that made her desirable, if not necessarily beautiful, and most of her job at the reservations desk involved fending off the advances of men, a task she was more than happy to perform. Sometimes they would wink at her and she would stare at them frostily. Sometimes they would slip her business cards along with their credit cards and she would make a conspicuous show of letting the business cards drop to the ground. Though sharply cynical and aggressively profane, Elsie was more timid than I was, especially in sexual matters, where she had a strict boyfriends-only policy. I didn't, and as I had moved my way through a series of brief affairs at the hotel, mostly with co-workers, occasionally with a guest, I had come to feel that my pleasure in the events was not complete until I had related them to her, shocking her a bit, watching her expression pass through shades of curiosity, envy, and satisfaction.

Elsie and I often talked about men, how needy and desperate they were without a woman on their arm and how unattractive they became once they had found that woman. We had seen this principle demon-strated repeatedly at the hotel. But that afternoon we were talking about science. Elsie had been a biology major in college, and both of her parents were doctors. Her decision to become a writer, she feared, had disap-pointed them both greatly; though they had not criti-cized her outright, their interest in her life diminished almost overnight. I understood perfectly—when I announced to my parents that I was going to take two years off after college to work, my father sighed audibly and hung up the phone. My mother was slightly more supportive—she stayed on the line and asked me questions about insurance and income taxes until *I* had to hang up the phone. "It's not that I don't like science," Elsie was saying. "I fucking love science. But I hate the idea of all the training. It's three more years of brain slavery, and then apprenticeship after apprenticeship after apprenticeship. People end up disconnected from the world, arrogant, greedy. Everyone I know who went to medical school fell victim to that shit. My parents don't really understand. They're both incorruptible."

"You could do something related," I said. "Go to work in a lab, or for a drug company."

"I've been thinking I should become a science writer," she said. "You know, for a newspaper. Explain medical discoveries to the public without totally mis-representing them. The other day I was working reservations and this woman checked in. She looked vaguely familiar to me, but she wasn't anyone I knew. Then I recognized her from the name on her credit card: she's that woman who writes science pieces for the *Post*. I think she's here for the conventions." That winter, the hotel was hosting two major medical conventions, which had been booked just two weeks apart, and many of the participants were staying for the entire month. The place was rotten with doctors.

"Well," I said, "did you talk to her? Maybe she could help you out: a little friendly advice for an ambitious young woman."

Elsie ticked a nail on the arm of her chaise longue. "I should have," she said. "I will. I have at least a week. And besides, she was with some guy who kept staring at me."

"Her boyfriend was putting the moves on you?"

"Yeah," she said. "In fact, he came back on his own with some lame question about the hours for the valet. It's so fucking stupid. This woman is perfectly pleasant and attractive. She's pretty. And her scumbag boyfriend is trying to fuck the help."

"Don't be so hard on yourself," I said. "And anyway, maybe you should sleep with him."

"Deborah!" Elsie said, her tone full of amplified scandal. "You want me to fuck her man out from under her? First of all, I have a boyfriend. Second of all, he has a girlfriend."

"Sooner or later you've got to give in," I told her. "Your self-control just isn't right. It's like you think that if you delay making mistakes as long as possible, you'll win."

"Won't I?" Elsie said. By the pool, women were laying out on their backs, balancing beers or piña coladas on their convex pink bellies. Brown men were getting browner in the sun. Arthur Manley was there, too, sitting in a chair near the deep end, reading a paperback book. In khaki shorts and a T-shirt, he didn't look like the man in the slate gray suit at all. He seemed like a much younger man, the kind of man who would come halfway across town to meet you for lunch just so you would agree to be his girl. "How about him?" Elsie said, pointing. "I saw you talking to him the other day."

"I only spoke to him once."

"He's a doctor."

"Really? He looks a little young."

"Doctors could be our age, more or less. That's why this is all so aggravating. I had better decide what I'm going to do, and do it quick."

"Do that guy," I said.

"I'm not doing that guy, or the other guy. I'm not going to fuck my way through the season."

"Don't you think he's a little handsome?"

"I think he's a little married," Elsie said.

"That's not true," I said, although of course it was.

I had seen the ring on his finger. It was the first thing I had looked for, and although I'm ashamed to admit it, my heart had sunk at the sight of the gold band.

"It is true. I've seen him with the same woman a bunch of times."

"What does she look like?"

"She's very short, about your height, and very blond. She looks a bit older than him. The two times that I've seen them, they haven't seemed so happy. Once they were eating in silence, and the other time she was complaining about something as they went into the elevator. I think she's a professor or something. She said something about a working vacation when they checked in."

"What floor are they staying on?"

Elsie smiled wickedly. "I'm afraid I can't disclose that information, ma'am."

"Tell me," I said.

She held up both hands.

"Ten?" I said.

"I give up," she said.

The next morning, I was straightening a small conference room off to the side of the lobby. My feet hurt, so I sat down and thought of Arthur Manley. Initially, I wasn't thinking about him as much as I was thinking about my life, and how the series of affairs that had punctuated my winter were beginning to wear on me.

It wasn't that I minded the rendezvous—I liked the excitement of them, the idea that something could still take my breath away—but I wondered more and more about whether I could spend more time with a man, whether I could be a girlfriend or even a wife. The furthest I had gotten in my own mind was mistress, an arrangement that seemed especially promising to me. I would see the man every week or so, we would share a bottle of champagne and a nice dinner, maybe catch a movie afterward, and then he would touch me everywhere. Then one of us would make a profession of love, and the other would protest, and the two of us would fall asleep together. He would love me, but he wouldn't be able to detach himself from his life. I would see the pain etched into his face. It would deepen our time together, make it resonate with romantic impossibility. I didn't have that in college, or in my two fruitless years of graduate school. I was the kind of girl who slept with her professors, or picked guys up at parties. I wasn't ashamed of it. It was sex. We went into a room and we made each other feel good. That was that. Still, the notion of being loved by a man, truly loved, so much so that it threatened to tear apart the fabric of his life, was a beautiful thing. I stood back up. My feet didn't hurt nearly as much, even after I cleaned for a while.

Later that week, I bumped into Arthur Manley as he

entered the main lobby, wearing the same slate gray suit and walking the same uneven walk. This time he came up and asked me if I would have a drink with him. "Sure," I said. We sat in a back corner of the upstairs bar, and I asked him questions about his job, and he asked me questions about mine. Not the hotel job, I mean, but my other job, the one where I was a struggling sculptor who had just completed a prestigious but not particularly lucrative commission for a Philadelphia public park. He was twenty-nine, three years older than me, and he lived in New York, where he was a first-year surgical resident at Columbia University Medical Center. He didn't say anything about a wife, and I didn't ask.

"Why do you have to work here?" he said.

"I don't have to," I said. "I want to. I don't have any of my sculpting materials with me—they're all at home—so it's more like a vacation. I make a little money. I read some books. I sketch new pieces. I sit out in the sun. And then I enjoy my spare time."

"I don't know what to do with mine," he said. At the bar's other tables, there were several couples composed of older men and younger women. Most of the older men had their arms around the younger women. I liked the idea that I was with a young man, and that he was leaning back in his chair, away from me. It meant that there was work to be done.

"I should go," I said. "But let's not make this the

last time." He smiled at me, and it was a different smile than the one he had given me before. This one was softer, more genuine, and it disappointed me somewhat. That night, I saw him and his wife standing in the lobby. She was as Elsie had described her—short and blond and voluptuous. She looked familiar to me, and later on I realized why: because she looked like me. We had similarly spaced features, similar short-bob haircuts, similar short legs that were solid to the point of being thick. I wondered if people could tell us apart from a distance. His hand was on her back, and he had an even softer smile on his face.

The more I thought about the prospect of an affair with Arthur Manley, the more likely it seemed. In fact, I realized that Arthur Manley and I were already in one of the rooms of the hotel, and that he was already lowering himself to the level of my hips, and sliding a hand between my legs, and whispering my name. It was only a matter of time. And since I couldn't stop time, it had in a sense already happened.

A few days later, a Palm Room bartender named Lucy quit to marry her boyfriend and move to Atlanta, and I added her shift to my housekeeping and greeting responsibilities. In four weeks, I had put more than three thousand dollars in the bank, and this would help me get near five thousand for my six-week run. From the first afternoon, I loved bartending. One afternoon a balding osteopath was trying to court me with bone jokes—one where an Indian medicine man calls the brachium the "breaky-um," another where the funny bone says to the humerus, "You have some nerve!" He was a little drunk, but he was good company, quick to smile and slow to judge. When Arthur Manley walked in, I thought that he was there to see me, but he took a seat beside the osteopath. "Doug," he said. "Long time no see." I moved away down the bar.

"Doctor," Doug said. "Can I buy you a drink?"

"No way," Arthur said. "But I can buy one for you. Where's the barmaid?"

"Right here," I said. "I'm the barmaid. But we're all bartenders now. It's the nineties."

"What's your name, bartender?" he said.

"This is Deborah," Doug said.

"Oh," Arthur said. "Do the two of you know each other?"

"Well, I've been entertaining the lady," Doug said.

"In that case," Arthur said, "maybe we should buy her a drink. Did he tell you the one about the humerus?" Doug giggled, and so did I. Arthur Manley beamed, as if he had just won something. On a bar napkin, he sketched some bones dancing in an ecstatic afterlife. It seemed to me that it might make a nice sculpture.

Later that evening, in the hallway leading back to the kitchen, Arthur kissed me for the first time, and slid his hand along the seam where my skirt met my blouse. And even later, he led me out behind the hotel and we went walking on the beach. The first hints of a rainstorm were coming down, but Arthur Manley said he didn't mind. "I'm always walking in the rain by myself," he said, "and this is just like that, except that you're with me." He moved briskly despite his strange crooked gait. I followed, laughing at anything that sounded like a joke. We didn't do much, just brushed the hair out of each other's eyes and stood within a few steps of the water. But it was the beginning.

After carrying on in this way—a steadily intensifying series of kisses and touches—for almost a week, I thought I should learn something about Arthur Manley's wife. The problem was that I didn't have any real way to proceed. I didn't want to ask Arthur directly. It seemed beside the point. And Elsie was no help.

Luck bailed me out. I was setting up for an afternoon shift at the bar when Arthur Manley's wife walked in. This time I got a closer look at her. I would describe her as a controlled woman, but even that is something of an understatement. She was tight around the eyes, and although there was considerable beauty in her face, she seemed not to notice it herself. She sat at the corner of the bar and arranged a fan of papers and books in front of her. I was wiping down the other end of the bar, but I was close enough to glance over at her, at the slightly worn black jacket and skirt, the new black mules, the silver necklace with a crescent-shaped charm at the end, the wedding band. After a little while, I went over. "Can I get you something?" I asked.

"Yes," she said, barely looking up from her work. "A Bloody Mary would be fantastic."

When I returned with her drink, I waited for her to look at me. I wanted at least that much. When she did, she had an expression that was a mixture of impatience and fear, and something about her face made me suddenly very fond of her. "What are you working on?" I said.

"Oh," she said. "It would only bore you."

"Try me."

"It's an article for an art history journal. I'm trying to figure out how nineteenth-century French etchings deal with small, personal objects. I'm having some trouble making the argument clear, even to myself."

I hadn't expected her to be so straightforward with her answer, so self-effacing and simple. "Personal objects? What, you mean like toiletries and things?"

"Sure. Hairbrushes, perfumes, jewelry, lingerie. Shoes are especially interesting. There's a long tradition in Flemish painting that invests all these things with meaning, but the French don't really have it until illustrators begin to come to prominence in the eighteen-forties." She picked at a loose thread on her

jacket. "Even though I'm not making it sound interesting, it is."

"Sounds like it," I said. "I'm an artist myself."
Another customer was signaling me; I ignored him.

"Really? What kind of work do you do?"

"I sculpt," I told her. The sentence hung there awk-
wardly, an obstruction. The other customer was
clearing his throat now. "I mean, I really do. I'm a
sculptor. Commissions for public places, mostly." I
heard an ashtray rattling against the tabletop. "I'm
sorry, though. I have to take care of this other customer." He was the kind of man who demanded
flirting with his drink order—he asked me what I
would do if he tipped real well—and by the time I had
dealt with him, Arthur Manley's wife was gone. I
hadn't even asked her name.

Elsie's boyfriend had been visiting her for the
weekend, so I hadn't seen much of her. This left me
more time to be with Arthur Manley, and more time to
be on my own, thinking about the pros and cons of
being with Arthur Manley. Saturday evening, Arthur
and I split a bottle of red wine in the Palm Room—I
was on the job—and then he invited me upstairs. "I
can't," I said. "It's not that I don't want to. It's that I
can't. But maybe tell me the room number, and maybe
sometime I'll see what I can do."

"It's ten thirty," he said. "But don't come by unannounced." He still said nothing about his wife.

By Monday, Elsie's boyfriend was gone, and the two of us were smoking on the patio again.

"So," I said, "how was Eric's visit?"

"Great. Well, good. It was nice to see him. Nice to fuck. But there are issues."

"Issues?"

"We're having trouble. There's some distance opening up."

"Problem distance? I mean, will it go away?"

"Not sure." She stubbed out her cigarette and immediately lit another one. "Listen, can I change the subject?"

"Go ahead."

"I talked to that science writer. She was leaving a spare key for a friend, and I told her that I knew her work, and we started talking. She said that she only has an undergraduate bio degree, just like me, and that she kicked around freelancing for almost ten years. She said that I should send her some of my work."

"That's great," I said.

"I guess," she said. "She also said that I should position myself as a medical writer rather than a science writer. Almost the same, but with more jobs available, because people are so preoccupied with their health."

"Yeah," I said. "Maybe you can debunk all this anti-smoking rhetoric."

"I'll do my best," she said. "First I need to practice a little bit more. So how about you? What have you been doing with yourself?"

"Well, I've been spending a little time with this guy."

"Which guy?"

"That guy we saw out here by the pool the other day."

"Deborah's been playing doctor," Elsie said with a snort. "I thought I was the medical writer."

"He's a nice guy."

"Has he given you a physical? Did he show you his stethoscope? Did he palpate? Has he been taking your temperature anally? I guess what I'm trying to say is, did you fuck him?"

"Okay," I said. "Now you've gone too far. We've just had a drink or two. Pleasant conversation. He seems like a nice enough guy."

"Has he mentioned his wife?"

"Not yet. You're sure he's married?"

"Absolutely. Or he's traveling with a hooker who is wearing a wedding ring. I've seen him with the same woman a bunch of times. Didn't I say that the last time?"

"Oh, well," I said. "That takes care of that." I tried to inject disappointment into my tone, and found to my surprise that it was already there.

My shift at the indoor bar dried up, and I got moved to poolside, which was much worse. The sun was too bright. There were too many kids making too much noise. The men who perched on the stools were generally ridiculous, either preeners and posers in their early twenties or dissolute alcoholics in their fifties and sixties. I preferred the alcoholics, who wore guayaberas and torn shorts and barely bothered to flirt with me, every once in a while making a halfhearted grab at my ass or telling me what they would do if they were twenty years younger. From the register, I could still see into the Palm Room, and what I noticed, apart from the fact that it was cool and dark and quiet, superior in every way to the poolside bar, was that Arthur Manley's wife was in there almost every day. She took the same seat at the corner of the bar and ordered Bloody Marys. She kept her head down over her papers while she drank, never lifting it to look around or talk to anyone.

On Friday, the hotel was bustling. The second medical convention was just about to begin, with a dinner dance, and the tuxedos and gowns were moving through the lobby. Elsie and I were working reception, and we could see into the ballroom through a slit created by the balustrade and a lobby pillar. Elsie kept leaving the desk to poke her head into the ballroom, after which she'd return with reports. "That old man with the mustache, the one who's always eating dinner alone, is dancing with a girl who absolutely fucking has to be a whore." That was followed by "There are two female doctors feeling each other up." Then she came and told me, "Your loverboy's in there dancing with his wife."

I went in to see. The song was a waltz, and Arthur Manley and his wife moved together perfectly, like two notes on a staff. They were more than two people dancing. They were a pair.

Midway through the waltz, Arthur stopped dancing and stepped away from his wife. She shook her head, more sadly than angrily, then turned on her heel and left. He followed. I followed, too, but at a safe distance, and when they got into the elevator I keyed myself into the freight elevator and rode up to the ninth floor, where I ducked into the B stairwell, and climbed the additional floor. Room 1030 was on the northeast corner of the hotel, right near the emergency stairs. If you stood in the stairwells, you could sometimes hear the conversation in the corner rooms. So that's what I did. I heard Arthur's wife screaming at him, something about her frustration at being trapped in a hotel with nothing to do. I thought you were working on an article, he said, and she answered that she was always working on something, but that she was sick of that being an excuse for him to ignore her. You can't understand, she said. I wonder about foolish things, about whether you still love me. A few moments later, I heard the sound of a woman murmuring, and then moaning.

Arthur and I were meeting for drinks most days now, although often we would go to another bar down the road. "Change of scenery," he said, "so you don't have to drink where you work."

"You mean poolside?" I said. "That's where I work now."

"Well, then," he said, "let's drink to forget."

For the first few weeks, we had practiced a kind of flirting that was generic but which I liked to think of as pure: he would say something funny or seductive, or repeat my name, or rub my shoulder while he nuzzled my neck. He didn't ask about my life and he didn't tell me about his. But time had pried him open slightly, and he had begun to introduce stories about his childhood. His father had been a Pittsburgh scrap-metal dealer in the war, and been successful enough to build a mansion in Squirrel Hill. He hadn't had Arthur until he was a very old man, and he had died while his son was still a boy. Arthur's mother had been an alcoholic, although the kind of sweet, supportive alcoholic who escaped detection until she lapsed into dementia while she was still in her early sixties. "My sister lives up near her," Arthur said. "She takes care of Mom. She's really great with her."

"What about your leg?" I said.

"Oh," he said. "Car accident when I was twenty-two. I was drinking and speeding. My fault, which is why I'm happy it was only my leg. Ever been in a wreck?"

"Every day of my life," I said.

He laughed and brushed my hair back from my forehead. "Poor baby," he said.

"You have no idea," I said, lying. Who wants to hear about a conspicuously uneventful life in the Baltimore suburbs that produced a reckless scorn for stability? Who wants to hear about parents who stayed together, a brother who loved me, a family that had lived in the same house for the past eighteen years, with the same brown leather couches and the same twenty-gallon fish tank?

One afternoon, Arthur and I went to a bar down the road and then took a quick drive. He was going to be away from the hotel for two days—a fishing trip down in the Keys, he said—so he was especially ardent, pulling the car into an alleyway and kissing me for a few minutes on the neck and upper arms before mounting his assault on the zippers and the buttons. When I got back to the hotel, there was a note in my box from Elsie to come and find her. "Guess what?" she said when I did.

"You quit smoking? Can I have whatever's left?"

She stuck out her tongue. "Guess who got Palm

Room afternoon shift?"

"The answer had better be me."

"Close," she said. "Me. But I'll swap you for pool-side if you want."

"I'm so fucking happy I could smoke," I said. "Join me on the patio?" We stood there and watched the water, how it moved and didn't move at the same time. "I should make a sculpture of the ocean," I said. I wasn't sure what I meant, but Elsie didn't seem to care. When the sun started to set, we pulled up chairs and sat down and felt the breeze come in.

The Palm Room was empty, so I made myself a gin and tonic and waited for business. I had a premonition about the first customer, and I was right: it was Arthur's wife. She was carrying a sheaf of papers and a big book, and she was dressed in jeans and the same black jacket. Beneath it I could see the puff of her belly. The affection that I had felt for her the last time we had spoken intensified. This woman, Arthur Manley's wife, was someone whose body I understood. She took her usual seat at the bar.

"I remember you," she said. "You sculpt."

"And I remember you," I said. "Bloody Mary?"

"Actually, my name is Nina," she said. After I brought her drink, she squared her papers in front of her. "Hey," she said. "I don't think you ever told me what your work is like."

"Little clay houses, and then I build landscapes for them out of sheet metal."

"Here in South Florida?"

"No. Up in Philadelphia."

"Really?" she said. "I have a friend who runs a small gallery there, and another friend who works at the Philadelphia Art Museum. You should give me a call when you get back up North." She handed me a business card. I slipped it into my purse, knowing I would never make the call.

"Thank you," I said.

"No problem," she said.

Then there was a long silence, during which she ran her finger over the lip of the glass. "Problems with the French?" I asked.

"I wish," she said. "That would be easy. I would just keep learning things until I had the answer. No, this is harder."

"What's wrong?" I said. She said nothing. "Hey, don't you have any respect for the bartender-as-therapist cliché?"

She smiled. "How old are you?" She stared at me. She couldn't possibly know. She wouldn't have been speaking to me this way if she did.

"Almost twenty-seven," I said.

"Get married right away," she said.

I laughed. "What?"

"You're young. Get married. You still have illusions

about love. Those illusions will protect you. In a few years that won't be the case." She fingered her wedding band. "This doesn't protect me at all." Her tone darkened. Did she suspect something after all? Or was she just staring at me the way you'd stare at any younger woman who bears some resemblance to yourself, as if you were staring into your own past and wondering when certain doors closed?

"From what?" I said. "Protect you from what?"

She didn't answer right away. "Well," she said. "It's hard to explain. The best metaphor I can come up with is water level."

"Bartender as therapist standing by for a better explanation," I said.

"There comes a time when you have to take a measure of the water level," she said. "You have to take a measure because the levels are dropping. There are two possibilties. Either it's just a matter of tides, and the tides will come back in, or it's leakage. If it's leakage, you have to find the source of the leak, or else you're finished. That's the drill. It's a little too pat, the way I've put it, but that's what you have to do."

There was another long silence. I kept wiping the tabletop, which had been clean for a while. "Well, if it's a leak, another drink might help."

"Thanks," she said. "I'll take a refill. But first, some other business." She gestured vaguely toward the bathroom. "Will you watch my papers while I'm gone?"

I watched them. In fact, I watched them closely; after I mixed her drink, I set it next to the papers and tried to read them upside down. I could pick out a few words here and there, *chien* and *chapeau*, but not much more. She had filled a legal pad with notes in a large, looped script: "Candleholders as symbols of consummated marriage…Private space versus public space…Most married women drawn without expressions, as if to render them all equal." The last line of the page said, "Medical devices: Arthur says." Arthur says? Did he help his wife with her research? Did she read him these articles when they were in bed? Did he love her for her work? I reached to turn the page and knocked over her Bloody Mary. Red slicked across the surface of the legal pad. "Shit," I said. I turned to grab a rag and turned back to find her standing in the doorway of the bar.

"I'm so sorry," I said. "I spilled your drink."

She looked stricken. "On the book?"

"No. On the pad."

"Oh, that's not so bad," she said. "I don't even think I filled out the first page."

"Let me clean it," I said. I tried to slide the articles out of the way, but I pushed too hard, and they fluttered to the floor. "God damn it," I said. "Ridiculous."

"Hey," she said. Her voice was stern but leavened by comedy. "Deborah. You come out here right now," she said. "I'll go back there. You've done enough damage."

I exited the bar at the corner and went to sit in her stool, dutifully, murmuring what an idiot I was. "Next drink's on me, obviously. And maybe the one after that."

She surfaced with papers in her hand. "As long as I'm back here, I'm going to drink whatever I want. Where do you keep the good vodka?" The sadness that had settled on her was gone. "I'll even make you a martini, if I can remember how."

"Fine," I said. "Everything's on the house."

When she came back out from behind the bar, I didn't move out of her stool. She sat down next to me. "I was thinking," she said.

"Very dangerous," I said.

"I was thinking that I take back the thing I told you about getting married."

"So now I should stay single?"

"Yes. Stay single forever. It's better. You have your freedom, right?"

"I guess I do. I'm not sure I use it as wisely as I should."

"I thought that was the point, to be unwise."

"It is, sometimes," I said.

"The thing about marriage is that it's both wonderful and horrible," she said. "My husband is a great person and also a selfish scumbag. He wants what's best for me and also only wants to please himself.

Forget about the disputes between people—marriage is all about the disputes within people." She emptied her drink. "Does that sound rehearsed?"

"A little," I said, because it did.

"Guess his name," she said.

"What?" I braced myself against the table.

"Guess my husband's name."

"Alan?" I said. Had I been drunker, I might have guessed correctly.

"No," she said. "It doesn't matter what his name is. My only point is that it's one of the only things about him that I really know for sure. I have spent so many years with him, and I have spent almost all that time trying to make sense of him. You know what he does?"

"How would I know?"

"Of course," she said. "He has this habit. He doesn't say 'I love you.' He never does. He says that it's too easy, that you see it in movies and on TV all the time. He says that it's been devalued over time. Instead, he says 'Adore.' Just the single word. He says it's our code, and that while everyone says 'I love you,' only two of us in the world are saying 'adore.' It's stupid, but that's the thing in my marriage that still means the most to me." After that, there wasn't much to say. When she climbed down from the stool, her movements had a heaviness to them, as if she was a much older woman. Which, of course, she was.

I knew where Arthur and I were headed. By now, we were spending entire afternoons on beds, rarely the same one, usually in vacant rooms on the thirty-fourth or thirty-fifth floors. I told him the higher floors were safer; the truth was, I was moving higher out of a mixture of ambition and escape. The altitude was erotic, as was his habit of unbuttoning my blouse, removing my bra, and looking at me before he undid his own belt, or before he nudged me back up against the headboard of the bed. Even though the point of our meetings was sexual, we weren't actually having sex yet—or, as Elsie would have said, we weren't fucking. He would touch me, of course, and sometimes I would put him in my mouth, but we didn't go any further. Any resistance to the idea was his; though I had met his wife and felt my full share of guilt, I was ready. Arthur, on the other hand, seemed to be slowing down the pace. Sometimes, he even bypassed sex entirely and opted instead for napping with me. Our conversations took on a certain sweetness. He would hold my hand and tell me about books he had read, or his dreams of one day giving up medicine and becoming a musician. Sometimes he would scribble little quizzes on pieces of paper: "Would you take a trip with me? Yes/No." He was like any other man, which is to say that he was like a boy. He needed more than anything to make himself known.

One day he came into the Palm Room. "Meet me

in my room at two," he said. "I can't say why, but you know why."

"You sure?"

"I'm sure," he said. "I've got everything covered."

In the room, at two, Arthur Manley was completely dressed except for shoes, and try as I might, I could see no shoes anywhere in the room. In addition, I saw scant evidence of his wife. She had nothing in the bathroom, and nothing on the counter. The only signs of her I saw were her black jacket hanging on the back of the desk chair, and a small picture of the two of them on the night table. "Who is this?" I said, holding the picture out to him. He was sitting on the bed reading a Graham Greene novel. One hand floated up to stroke my hip.

"Me and my wife." He looked at me. "You're not surprised, I expect."

"No," I said. "Well, a little. I mean, you could have mentioned it to me."

"Yes," he said. "I should have."

"Where is she now? New York?"

"No. She's here with me."

"Here?" I raised my voice. "Here in the hotel, the whole time that we've been…" The indignation was a joke, of course, a joke I wanted him to get. He got it.

"Yep," he said jauntily. "The whole time. Anyway, that says more about her indifference to my life than it does about my insensitivity. We're having a lot of trouble these days."

"She's very pretty," I said.

"She looks like you." Arthur Manley fixed me with a strange expression that was pitched halfway between a smile and a grimace, and I thought that maybe I had underestimated him. Then I was sure that I had underestimated him, because the next thing he did was ask me to take off all my clothes and put on his wife's jacket. I couldn't refuse. I was as fascinated with the idea as I would have been with a murder scene.

While Arthur was in the bathroom, I went rooting through the nightstand. That's when I found his wife's wedding ring. It was the same one she had been wearing in the bar, and I wondered why she wasn't wearing it, wherever she was. Then I turned it in the light, and then I put it on. I was hoping Arthur wouldn't notice. He rarely looked at my hands.

I was sitting on the floor, and he came and sat beside me. He flashed a smile at me, but it wasn't the kind smile I had seen him use with his wife on the dance floor, or even the paternal smile he had flashed during the conversation with Doug. This was a hard smile, a fast smile, the smile I remembered from our very first meeting. It was the smile I had been waiting for. "What if I told you I loved you?" he said. His eyes were a symphony of demands.

"Don't you dare," I said.

He took me there on the floor, from behind, while I wore his wife's jacket and wedding ring. I cannot help it that this seems staged, pornographic, or melodramatic. It was not any such thing at the time. I couldn't have predicted it, not exactly, and then it happened, and I was like a cat lucky enough to have a canary fall from the sky at its feet. This room had smoked-glass mirrored doors on the closets, like all the rooms at the Grand Palms, and an original piece of art, which was an abstract that looked like a corridor of pebbles. My pleasure built very quickly, in fifteen minutes at most, and then I came powerfully, twisting back against his chest, and pushing forward into the carpet, clutching, moaning. Remember, this is just an objective report; if I had laughed or wept or suffered a dizzy spell, I would report that, too. I came again when he turned me on my back and spread my legs, and once more as I watched my own hand stiffen into a claw. It was the hand with the wedding band.

When Arthur went to wash, I slipped the ring into the pocket of the black jacket, where I was sure his wife would find it.

Afterward, we both knew that things were different. He piled my hair on top of my head and looked at me for a long time. Neither of us spoke. Then he scribbled something on a piece of paper, folded it, and handed it to me. On top, he had written, "If you are the kind of woman who trifles with a man's emotions, please walk out this door." Next to that he had drawn a door. Underneath that, he had written, "If you know what you want, how you feel, and what kind of life you have welling up inside you, then please walk this way." And next to that he had drawn an arrow pointing up into the text of the note, beyond it, toward him.

I took the pen from him and drew an arrow to the picture of the door. "Adore," I wrote, and then turned and left the room. It was the cleverest thing I had ever done, and the cruelest, and also the kindest.

Signs

Right off the bat I knew there was an issue. "Right off the bat" is not exactly a baseball term but it could be. Baseball has a bat and sometimes the ball comes right off it. "On the ball" is similar. Baseball has a ball. But right off the bat I knew there was an issue is what I am saying. All you had to do was look at the sign to know it. "Peseason Ends Satuday," it said in black plastic letters four inches tall. "Get Ready for the Regular Season." The problem had nothing to do with the number of Rs available in the letter set. The problem was me.

I was in charge of maintaining all the signs in the stadium complex. Some of them were letter-by-letter. Some were word-by-word. Some of them were slide-outs, where the whole thing was a translucent sheet and the old sheet got thrown out and a new one came in. It was not always an easy job, as an understanding of spelling and punctuation were required, but it was not a difficult job either. Dennis, my boss, wanted me to finish up with the preseason sign and get to work on the displays above the gift-shop jewelry cases. They were slide-outs. "Watches were last season's golden boy," he said. "Now pendants carry the day."

I didn't know about getting to work on the jewelry slide-outs. I was not performing to the best of my ability. At my feet was a sign that said, "All shoes 30 percent off." It replaced a 20 percent off sign from the week before. The deep discount was a result of an overproduction of signature shoes in the previous season and an underproduction by the first baseman who had lent his name and signature to the model. That sign was perfect. But the preseason sign was a disaster and I could not dispute that. It was an error on my part. That is a baseball term: an error. I sat down on the small bench seat behind the sign stand. At that moment, she called me on the cell. "Hi," she said.

"Hold on," I said. I walked from the sign stand to the window of the gift shop, where two attractive female mannequins were modeling caps and jerseys.

"You know," she said. "You're a dumbass. You suffer from a lack of will and motivation. Oh, also, you're ungainly." She laughed a tinkling laugh that was like a crack that spreads in spiderwebby fashion over a pane of glass. "Do you know what 'ungainly' is?" she said. "It's clumsy and ugly. You are both!"

"Where are you?" I said.

"In my father's apartment in the skybox," she said. "I'd have you up, but you're clumsy and ugly and talking too much for my tastes!"

Her father had been a military man and then a businessman. He stood six foot three. If I were making a sign describing him, it would read "A dealership- and team-owning man." The first hyphen, the one after "dealership," would point into empty space. This was called a suspensive hyphen and it was important to know for signmaking. The dealership was a car dealership, and he had used the money from that to buy a partial interest in the team. His favorite baseball player of all time was George Brett, who had played for the Kansas City Royals and, in 1980, approached the magical benchmark of a .400 batting average before falling off late in the season. Brett's middle name was Howard, which was also her father's first name. I asked her what her father would think of these phone calls.

"My dad?" she said. "My dear old dad? You mean, would he care that I'm calling from his skybox?"

"No. I mean would he approve of how you treat me?"

"Of course not. He'd chastise me. He treasures the idea of you because you treasure his little girl. Of course my dad's favorite aircraft is the F-117 Nighthawk, which never exactly raised the bar on airborne grace. During daylight hours, it had to hide from Soviet satellites, so you know what they nicknamed it? The Cockroach. Sometimes that's how I think of you."

It was making me nervous, talking to her. Dennis, my boss, was paying me good money to make and hang signs. Dennis was her uncle. Her family was too much in my life, in too many directions. Dennis's favorite baseball player was Dave Concepción, who had played for the Cincinnati Reds in the seventies and eighties, showed only moderate talent at the plate but quick feet on the base paths, and enjoyed one of his best seasons when he was thirty-nine years old, batting .319. I did not have a favorite baseball player, although I admired and even had some affection for Jerry McNertney, Bob Kearney, Oddibe McDowell, Lou Berberet, Jerry May, Harry Chiti, Daryl Boston, Marvin Benard, Lee Walls, Rube Manning, Rube Vinson, and Rube Waddell.

"Hey." She was still on the line. "You upset?"

"Me? No."

"Don't lie to me. You have to be straight with me."

"I'm not upset."

"So maybe you're not upset. Maybe you're just not excited to talk to me. Is that possible?"

"It's possible."

"Do you want me to apologize so you can get more excited?" she said.

"No," I said. "That's okay. No apology necessary."

"Oh," she said. "Please. I mean, can I please apologize to you? I'm so sorry. Me apologize long time.

You're right to be hurt. You are in pain. Who can you blame for your pain? My dad blames the powerhouses in the American League. My uncle blames leading economic indicators. Who is your cross to bear?"

"I have to go," I said. "I have to hang a shoe-discount sign. They're thirty percent off now."

I reached to hang up. The breasts of the mannequins ennobled me. "Wait," she said. "I have nothing on. My clothes are scattered across the floor. I can see them all. Pants, shirt, underwear, bra. Like I said, I'd have you up if you weren't so stupid."

We first met in the skybox. Dennis was hosting a party for new employees. It was held on June 17, which was the birthday of Dave Concepción. When I arrived at the party, she was sitting in a plush chair that was covered with a cloth that was decorated with a floral pattern. She wore extremely high-heeled shoes and a short skirt and a smile that some people would call mysterious. She also had a shirt on, but I don't remember anything about it other than that it was on and that I wished that it weren't. "You're one of the imbeciles who works for my uncle?" she said. "If his employees got any stupider he'd qualify for federal funding." Though I didn't know it at the time, this indicated an interest. Two hours later I knew. I was taking off my pants and she was kneeling next to me with her shirt still on. "You cleared the fences," she said. That was a baseball term.

I was her second man of the day, that day we met. Earlier, she had been in the museum looking at paintings by an artist whose name I did not know. "You don't know him?" she said. "His work is in permanent collections in London, Paris, Rome, Moscow, Lisbon, Stockholm, Perth, Mexico City, Lamisil, and Winnetka." She had said the same exact thing in the museum, and the man standing beside her was besotted by her knowledge regarding the artist. She let him coax her back to his hotel, where he took her shirt off in the stairwell and began to touch her at various points. She was excited by what were occurring. She was also strangely unaffected. She cast her head back in a simulation of passion. It was all she could do, as there was something missing in her that prevented her from being emotionally involved in the moment. "In any moment," she said. She was, she explained, like a cloud capable of imitating the shapes of other clouds, but not capable of rain. This was uncharacteristically poetic for her, which suggested to me that she was truly upset. She promised she would never fake anything with me: misery, ecstasy, disinterest.

On the phone, in the stadium, I remembered this, and I asked her. "Remember when you said you would never fake anything with me?" I said.

"Yes."

"That was a long time ago. Have you?"

"No."

"It seems like it sometimes."

"Well, I'm faking faking," she said. The explanation was utterly convincing. "Will you come up here now? I have changed my mind. I need to see you. Come now. I will make it worth your while." She then used several baseball terms including "dugout," "warning track," "slider," and "corked bat." It seemed like she was challenging me to interpret her mood.

Now let me say something about signs. Signs say something. Letters and symbols these days are produced by computers and cut by machines that cost hundreds of thousands of dollars. They are backed by peelable adhesive and are pressure-sensitive and are easy to apply to any relatively smooth, nonporous surface, whether reflective or nonreflective.

Now let me say something else about signs. There are signs in baseball also, though they are not letter-by-letter signs or word-by-word signs. Catchers make them with their fingers to suggest to pitchers what to throw and first- and third-base coaches (again, the suspensive hyphen) sometimes develop complex signs to communicate with base runners.

Now let me say something that is not about signs. I burst through the skybox door and then the second door that led to the private bedroom. We had a ball. She cast her head back in a simulation of passion, and she was sad to have to lie.

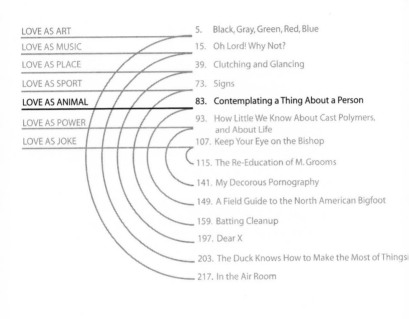

Contemplating a Thing About a Person

Contemplating a thing about a person is what I was doing or rather trying to do when a dog trotted past me and crapped on the sidewalk. A policeman took out his gun. It was impenetrably gray, like someone's unheard prayer. The policeman lifted his gun, pointed it at the dog, and told the dog that it would soon be in heaven, pursuant to county code section seven subsection twenty-eight. The dog looked at the policeman with a calm it probably did not feel and then walked off down the street. The policeman put up his gun and I got back to the business of contemplating a thing about a person.

The person was Geraldine, whose name I wanted to push off a cliff. "You can't change it?" I said to her every time I saw her, and every time she replied that she could change it, but that then she would be changing everything. It would be like a statue coming to life to unscrew and replace the brass nameplate at its base. I did not understand her metaphor but I liked the way it moved from Point A to Point B but I did not like the way it turned our conversation away from the issue of her name.

Her name stayed the same no matter how many times I challenged it and each time after her refusal to change it she showed me something. It was something she had. I forget the word for what she had exactly. Charisma? Eros? A nice tight rug of muscles in her back? I forget.

Geraldine sat on a porch. It was attached to her house. "Attachioed," she said, "like mustachioed." One word would have done fine but three was even better. I had stopped by to see her and was about to take the walk that would bring me the dog and the policeman. Coffee was in my stomach and the memory of the morning newspaper's headlines was in my mind. My eyes were puffy behind sunglasses. I had been up late, you see, contemplating.

"Hey, Sunglass Hut," Geraldine said. "It's too warm for a jacket." She wore a slip dress that had been designed by a young man from New York City. He had been a close friend of her brother's before a period of great unfriendliness intervened, and he had mailed the dress to Geraldine in an attempt to win back her brother's goodwill. It was yellow and sheer and showed off many things including probably the thing I was contemplating.

"I can't argue with you there," I assured her. My jacket wasn't quite heavy enough to infuriate her so I went off without incident. Twenty minutes later a dog and a gun and a policeman assembled into an anecdote that I have already partially related and which I will soon bring to its fascinating conclusion.

When the dog crapped on the sidewalk, the smell was pretty much unmentionable. Geraldine had a way of describing bad smells. She said that they "smelled like they came from nature."

The policeman showily put his gun up. He slid a finger across the patch on the front of his uniform and announced who he was. "Policeman," he said.

I went around the block in the direction the dog had gone but when I turned the corner I didn't see it. I was contemplating Geraldine's head. She had a lovely large head that resembled a child's drawing of the sun. She herself referred to it as a "pumpkin head," and no one saw fit to disagree, except behind her back, where they wondered if it was not in fact slightly larger than a pumpkin. A wise man once said that a duck is a chicken that speaks Chinese. I can't speak to that but I can say that a large head isn't much of a drawback for a woman because it can contain, in addition to a large smile, large expressive eyes. Geraldine also had large breasts and legs that remained shapely right down to the feet. She was immensely attractive and had recently begun to explore the idea of opening a restaurant whose floor plan would be based on the spiral, a shape that had obsessed her since she was an eight-year-old girl. She knew what kind of food the place would serve but she wouldn't tell me. "Let's plug into that old blue amp and rock out until dawn," she said by way of not quite answering. This was some kind of come-on and I was more than happy to have it on the books.

I went around the block in record time and when I returned to the spot where the dog had crapped on the sidewalk the crap was still there. That was no surprise. What was a surprise was that the dog was also there, dead, stretched out next to the crap in a sad brown crescent. Blood came out of him in a skinny descender and trickled nearly to the crap.

When I saw the dead dog and the dog crap and the string of blood that connected them I ran back to Geraldine. I didn't know where else to go. She was still on the porch and I called to her to put her shoes on and come down to save me from what I had seen. To save me, she said, she'd have to see it also. To get to that point we had to ignore everything along the way. We wanted to keep our minds pristine for what would certainly be our undoing. We ignored the hand-painted sign that said "Praise God Who Has Put Rocks in Your Pockets." We ignored the man on the corner who was humming Bach and the man next to him who was humming Shvantz. We ignored the magic picture in the window of the Chinese restaurant that showed a waterfall running backward. We ignored the buzz that rose out of the gym where they held afternoon fights. Liberty was kicking the marrow out of Justice. Equality had taken one on the chin from Fraternity. That much was clear from the noise of the crowd.

We arrived at the crap site.

"You're an idiot," Geraldine said. "There's no dog here."

"Maybe the policeman took him away." I bad-mouthed him frantically. "Or maybe he killed the dog and had to move him to cover his tracks."

"But then there would be a chalk outline of a dog. There's no chalk outline. Do you see one? I don't."

The story of the dog had ended abruptly, and not at all like I wanted it to end. I had imagined that Geraldine would stand beside me, soaking up the chilling sight of the crap, the dog, and the blood, and, faced with this tableau of life and death, draw ever nearer to me, perhaps even softening to the idea of changing her name. But she was only certain that she had been taken for a ride. She stepped away from me. Her face had gone flat. I thought that maybe the problem was that I had been drinking too much coffee, which sometimes made my breath smell like it came from nature. We went to a bench and sat down. "I need to tell you something," she said. "Do you remember when I was sitting on the porch?"

"Do I ever," I said.

"Well, then you must remember that I was looking pretty good, and feeling even better."

"You said it."

"This is a nice slip dress and it felt nice in the breeze on the porch."

"You're not just whistling Dixie."

"My friend Eric came by this morning and sat with me, and it was clear that he liked the way I looked."

"Clear as day."

"I liked that he liked the way that I looked."

"What's not to like?"

"I don't feel well often enough to ignore it." I couldn't think of anything to say. She went on. "But here is where my question comes in."

"Fire away."

"Why would you take me away from that? To see nothing and then sit on this bench thinking about nothing?"

"It wasn't nothing."

"It wasn't anything," she said. "You can see from here."

Leaning out from the bench but not standing up I tried to see but could not. I had lost the grain of the sidewalk.

We sat. She said nothing and I was kind of in that

mood, too. Another policeman came by on patrol but this one was quite a different matter, with coarse features that were to be frank canine and a handlebar mustache of the deepest blue-black. Geraldine looked at him, knowing full well that he was not the policeman who had killed the dog, and all at once she began to cry. "I don't know," she said. "Maybe it is something. I just don't know." Her lovely large head rolled around tearfully. The policeman did not stop to look and I was glad. It was none of his business. It was not a pretty sight. It was a beautiful one.

How Little We Know About Cast Polymers, and About Life

On the day that the Hospice Pathetic died, I was reading about genetically modified linseed plants. Created by scientists in a laboratory environment, the plants accumulated high levels of very long chain polyunsaturated fatty acids in seed. This was good news, you see, because prior to the appearance of these engineered oils, the most reliable source for very long chain polyunsaturated fats was fish, and wild and farmed fisheries were straining to meet increased global demand. Now, with the help of science, we could get the oils from linseed plants. It was a miracle, or so the scientists in the article said. To be honest, I didn't really care. I was reading about the oils only because it was the lead article in the in-flight magazine. I would have rather read about the Hospice

Pathetic. Matters of life and death interested me greatly. Still, I made do with what was available to me; I returned to the article and learned several additional interesting facts about very long chain polyunsaturated fatty acids.

I was traveling from New York City to Boston, where I had a four-hour layover, and then I was going on to Mexico City, then to Stockholm, then to Tallinn. If this seems roundabout, it was. I was a spy. I can't tell you what government agency I was working for, or whether or not my mission involved assassinating a foreign dignitary in the Boston airport, or whether I was traveling under the name "Rodolfo Pilas" and affecting a slight Spanish accent, or even if anything in this paragraph is true, except for the thing about the linseed plants, and even that might, in theory, be a code that I'm using to send a message to certain people who would, let's say, need to know how to assemble a certain piece of equipment, like some fancy gyroscopic circuit that's being used in a cutting-edge missile-location system that would, if it fell into the wrong hands, wreak havoc on what little bit of peace we have left in the modern world.

In theory.

So, there I was, reading about linseed oil, wondering how the Hospice Pathetic felt—if she felt anything at all—hovering in the space between existence and nonexistence. Before I go any further, let me make sure that we are talking about the same Hospice Pathetic. She was a Florida woman who collapsed in her midtwenties after years battling eating disorders, suffered severe brain damage as a result of that collapse, went along in that brain-damaged state for more than fifteen years, and then became the center of a national controversy when her husband, who was also her court-appointed guardian, argued for her feeding tube to be removed, insisting that he was acting in accordance with her previously articulated wishes. Though her parents immediately objected to the decision, their appeal was rejected, and as the Hospice Pathetic neared death, her case was taken up by all manners of politicians and activists. The governor of Florida and even the United States Congress tried to intervene. They believed they had a right to promote life, and that those who supported her husband's attempt to remove the tube were promoting death. The Hospice Pathetic was, for the last weeks of her life, the center of intense media scrutiny as she lay largely immobile in her bed. She had a name, of course, but I called her the Hospice Pathetic, both to protect her privacy and to illustrate the way in which her personal identity became secondary to her use as a political symbol.

In theory.

I can't say any more, to be perfectly honest. I may have information about the case, or a person or persons involved in the case, that would reflect badly on other people—people in power—and that's why I'm relieved that I have at least something to report from that long day of traveling. It is a distraction, a story about traveling, but it can be a compelling distraction, especially when it could possibly involve a man clasping his hands together, saying "Madre de Dios," humming a snatch of the Carmina Burana, and then moving his hands to the back of his head, where instinct led him to believe that he might catch whatever blew out.

But I am getting ahead of myself.

A slight cold was beginning to fog my head as I read the linseed article. This was a shame, because I still had many miles and many hours to travel on what I should probably describe as "a little trip taken by an Spanish-American cast polymer manufacturer seeking new business partners in Estonia." I had never been to Estonia, or at least there was no record of my ever having been there. I was looking forward to drinking some local vodka and maybe making the acquaintance of a young lady, ideally paid, in the moody, somewhat threadbare hotel where I would be staying courtesy of the United States government—or, to be more circumspect, courtesy of Mar-Corp, a leader in supplying synthetic marble surfaces to Southern California contractors since 1989.

The idea of watching a long, young Estonian girl slip out of bed as I hovered on the border between sleep and waking both aroused and saddened me. I had done too much thinking about the link between youth, beauty, and death. I sighed as I screwed the silencer onto my gas blowback Maruzen Walther P99. I was in the bathroom stall, which never quite felt dignified, but it's one of the only places in an airport where you can have your gun out. I glanced at the tiles and wondered if they might not look better in synthetic marble.

From the bathroom, I went to the newsstand. "Excuse me," I said to an attractive young redhead standing by the financial magazines. "Did you by any chance grow up in San Diego?"

She looked up at me, took a beat, and beamed. "Mr. Pilas," she said. "Hello. Yes. I'm Jennifer Lee. I was friends with your son David."

"I thought so," I said. "How are you?"

"Good," she said. "And David?"

"Good," I said. "He's married. Just had his first child."

"I had heard that there was a baby on the way. So you're a grandfather? Congratulations."

"Thank you," I said.

"Say hi to David," she said. "I actually have to go. My plane's boarding in a minute."

"Nice to see you." It *was* nice to see her. A certain quantity of necessary information had been conveyed to me in an efficient clandestine manner.

I went to the gate. If I had a target, I was expecting to see him pass through the lobby in exactly twelve minutes, wearing a brown leather jacket, which isn't to say that I had a target at all. I opened up my laptop computer to a rather anonymous-looking spreadsheet. If I had been asked, I would have said that I was figuring out wholesale prices for adhesive-backed waterproof tiling. I would have said it apologetically, as if I could not help but furnish excessive specifics in the vain hope of making a boring subject at least ironically interesting. "You know how things are with adhesive-backed waterproof tiling," I would have said. "No one likes to think about it, but people depend upon it every day."

Next to me two men were talking. The one closer to me was short and bald; the one farther away was taller and wore a knit cap. They were in their early thirties and they were clearly close friends.

"I read an article that bothered me," the first one said.

"Yeah?" said the other.

"It's just those liberal magazines," the first one said. "I know you probably agree with everything they say, but they make me mad."

"Tell me why," the second one said. I searched his face for sarcasm. I am practiced at detecting any kind of disjunction between what is said and what is felt. Sometimes it means the difference between life and death. In this case, the man seemed to have a genuine interest in what his friend was saying.

"Well, you know, even knowing about the bias ahead of time, I was quite disappointed with how they covered the case." They were talking about the Hospice Pathetic. Everybody was.

"Bias in what sense? You're not one of those people who secretly thinks that liberals wanted her to die, are you?"

"I don't secretly think anything. Look, as far as I'm concerned, there are only two real issues in the case: what she wanted to happen to her if she was ever brain-dead, and whether or not she was really brain-dead at the time the decisions were being made." He put his hands out on his lap and folded them formally. "Let's start with the first. I believe that there is strong reason to doubt what she actually wanted. I find it difficult, though not impossible, to believe that she told her husband at the age of twenty-three, or twenty-five, that she would rather die than be in a persistent vegetative state. So her wishes are in question, right?"

"But wait," the second man said.

"Let me finish," the first man said. "Please let me finish. I have heard you go on defending your candidates, attacking the president. Can I finish?"

"Sure," the second man said. "Finish."

"The second issue, of course, is whether or not she is in a persistent vegetative state. Again, I don't know.

It is well known that the diagnosis is very difficult. Why not allow another neurologist to examine her? Some things don't add up. For example, a major criterion of the persistent vegetative state is the complete lack of awareness of pain. If she is in that state, then why has her physician been giving her morphine? I think we need more certainty. I think that without it, these activists' courts are possibly sanctioning, if not committing, murder."

I glanced at my watch. I had eight minutes left until my target was scheduled to approach. His movements would seem to him to be an exercise of his free will, but they were in fact choreographed by an organization much larger than he could imagine. The taxicab that picked him up from his hotel, for example, was outfitted with tiny, nearly undetectable heaters that would subtly dehydrate him on his way to the airport. Once inside the airport, he would proceed to the first kiosk, where he would purchase a bottle of water. You could say that there was a good chance of this occurring, but the fact is that there was a certainty of this occurring. Habits had been studied, special signage created, and so forth. The probability was so high that it was almost godly. Thanks to a miniature delivery system mounted on the engagement ring of the cashier at the snack kiosk, the water he was sold would have been dosed with a powerful time-release diuretic. This additive would take effect exactly three

hundred seconds later, when—if his foot speed held—
he would be twenty yards away from the entrance to a
bathroom. I would follow him into the bathroom, at
which time janitorial personnel would instantly block
off the entrance. Inside, at the urinals, I would come
up behind the man, ask him to kneel, and then discuss
manufacturing advances in synthetic marble tile. I can
say no more.

The gate area was strangely silent, despite the
announcements overhead, and after a few seconds, I
realized why: I no longer heard the two men next to
me talking. I turned to look at them. The second man
was staring at me. My blood chilled around my bones.
I had been lost in thoughts of my plan, and I had violated the first rule of my profession, which was to
remain vigilant. Was the man another spy? I tightened
my hand around my Walther.

"You know," the second man said to his friend. "I
can't say you're wrong, though I know you're not right.
I've been ignoring the issue as best as possible for a
number of reasons, chief among them the fact that
there's no way to really know anything in this case. At
this point, the situation has been so politicized that it's
become more about grandstanding than about anything else. I'm sure her husband doesn't remember
exactly what she said. Who would? But a better question is this: who else would? For that matter, what difference does it really make? This is a private dispute

that the courts helped to settle. The rest of this is toxic, as far as I'm concerned. I don't like seeing her case, in life or death, be used for further divisiveness. It's just not a clear enough example, with enough legitimate facts, for there to be anything smart said about it."

My grip on the gun relaxed. The two men sat facing one another wordlessly for a moment. Their disagreement, civil as it was, had put something between them. When they got up to leave, I checked my watch again. Four minutes to target. Time sped up. Two minutes. One minute. And then he was there, younger than I had expected, his walk full of a life that he would not have for long. I followed him into the bathroom; I introduced myself; he exchanged what he thought was the proper set of code words; he accepted the appearance of the Walther with equanimity at first, convinced that it was merely a precaution; he even knelt without much resistance; at the click of the hammer his hands flew up to cover the back of his head; I ended the sentence with indisputable punctuation.

Coming out of the bathroom, I went down the concourse to a bar to have a beer—I always liked to have a beer before I left America. The news was about the Hospice Pathetic. She had died. Her fate was inevitable and yet it affected me profoundly. I dabbed at my eyes with a napkin and I was not the only one there who did so. Some of the others were men, too.

The nearest one to me said that he was a grandfather from Kansas. "I didn't know exactly how to feel about this," he said. "It was bad on every side." I nodded. "What's the world coming to?" he said. I told him about linseed oil and that improved his mood. "Sounds great for a landlocked state like Kansas," he said. "When I get home tonight, I'm going to tell my grandkids that they're going to live forever."

I had another beer and headed back toward the plane. On my way I saw the two men from the gate, walking toward me. They had evidently not yet made their peace. They stood apart from each other, and as they came closer to me, I saw that their expressions were less friendly than before. They got closer. The short man was on my left. The tall man was on my right. They were still angry enough with one another to let a stranger walk through the middle of them. I pulled nearly even with them. The short man grabbed my left arm. I went for the Walther, but the tall man had already put a needle in my right shoulder. I could not move, but the tall man was strong enough to keep me upright, at least long enough until we had gone through a door and were in a large, bare room. The tall man did not say anything. The short man reached inside his jacket while he whistled Carmina Burana.

Keep Your Eye on the Bishop

From Capistrano the swallows come. To Capistrano they return. I'm sure there is a joke there.

Did you hear the one about the rabbi and the Catholic priest who walked into a garment factory? They turned toward one another and said, "Our religions are immaterial." Then the priest goosed the rabbi.

She told me this joke. In fact it was not this joke but one somewhat like it. But I am honor-bound not to repeat her joke. Why? Because she said she was tired of being erased—or, more to the point, of being written. "Everything I say ends up elsewhere," she said on the telephone. "I'm like a footnote in everyone else's story."

"Hold on," I said. "Talk slower so I can get this all down. It's great stuff."

"You're a jerk," she said. "Can't you take this seriously?"

"Can't…you…take…this…seriously."

"I'm done. I have said enough."

"You have not said enough."

"Enough."

"Not enough."

On we went, into the night. A bird fell out of the sky from exhaustion. The word "enough" wobbled in my mind until it began to look funny, like an overly formal portrait of someone you see every day.

On we went, into the morning.

I wish I could explain the pain involved in this process of rootless badinage and deferred intimacy.

I shot myself in the foot once. It felt like that until I realized that it was in fact someone else's foot. Ha ha. So be it.

Here is another joke. According to the constitution and canons of the Episcopal Church, a majority of bishops with jurisdiction must ratify an election. One day, on the eve of an election, one particular bishop called the secular press and the church media to make an announcement. "I am fearful that I cannot truly connect with another human being," he said. "Sometimes I will sit across a table from someone and wish that I could be close to that other person, not just at that moment, but at other moments. I wish that I could set aside my petty rages and my impeding fears. When the swallows return to Capistrano they are stating their connection to the place. It is a recurring, powerful, natural connection, as much poetry as it is instinct, as much faith as it is nature. But I cannot achieve that and so my heart remains imprisoned." The reporters roared. They thought he was playing the fool, even when he froze in his sorrow and his shame and could say no more.

She calls to say we should go for Baloopian food.

"What's that?"

"Like Chinese. But from Baloopia."

"Ah, Baloopia."

"I almost went there on a trip once."

"Did you? What year?"

"Ninety-four."

"I was all over Europe in ninety-three. Crazy to think we could have run into each other in Baloopia. Although we didn't know each other then."

"We didn't. That's true."

"But we do now."

"I can't hear you. My air conditioner is loud."

"What?"

"Exactly. So loud I feel like saying 'What?' all the time. Nice joke."

"I wasn't making a joke. I could hear you. I just didn't understand why you mentioned the air conditioner."

"Why wouldn't I mention it? It's loud. Isn't that what you do to the loudest thing in the room? Mention it?"

"And that thing is your air conditioner?"

"Louder than a bomb."

"Talking to you makes me hungry."

"I'm not sure you're allowed to say that."

"Why not?"

"Because of what it suggests."

"But you're allowed to talk about Baloopia any time you like?"

"Sure," she said. "It's a place. Places get talked about sometimes. It's very different from what you're doing. What you're doing, my friend, is sketchy."

The telephone line filled with an embolism of silence.

The bottom was about to fall out of our banter, and I knew it. I knew that the things I was saying were, if not wrong, at least risky, and a tiny fraction of me wished that I could control myself. But then there was the vast majority, and I am a democrat of me.

I hung up with a complaint about the air conditioner.

That night I had a dream. I was in a glass cage suspended over the street. People were walking by below, and I was screaming for them to look up at me, but no one could hear. There was a woman who looked kind of like her, and I shouted and shouted, but she wouldn't turn around. She was deep in conversation with a man who was holding a handwritten sign identifying him as the president of the United States. In the dream, I understood. You can't expect anyone, even a woman of your acquaintance, to pass up a chance to talk to the president of the United States.

I told her a joke. This I can report. There was a man and he was rooting through a closet looking for a pair of old shoes when he found a box. "What is this box?" he said to his wife.

"Don't touch," she said. "The box is mine."

A few days later, his wife was out and the man found himself with a growing curiosity about the box. He opened it and saw that it contained four eggs and one thousand dollars. The man waited until his wife was home and confronted her about the box.

"I told you not to touch my box," she said.

"Will you explain it to me?" he said. "Please?"

Through her anger she did so. She told him that every time they had bad sex she would put an egg in the box. He did not say anything but he was secretly pleased. In ten years of marriage, only four eggs? "What's the money?" he said.

"Oh," she said. "Every time I got a dozen eggs, I sold them."

When I told her this joke, she laughed, then said, "That's not funny," then said, "You're stupid," then laughed again. All the while the light played upon her face.

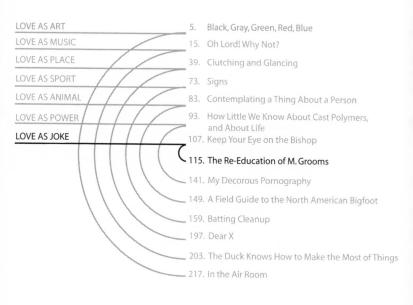

The Re-Education of M. Grooms

We reupped our top show at the eleventh hour. I thought for sure it was beyond our means, but then our lawyer spent an evening in a bar uptown with their lawyer, sidecar led to sidecar, and we got another season of *Chop Circus* for a song.

"Isn't that great?" said Rose, the secretary at the network whose white bun and sunny disposition had greeted me every morning for fifteen years. "It's like another year of life." That's exactly what it was, although I didn't have the heart to tell her it was a mixed blessing.

Listen: There have been times when I was everything to life and life was everything to me. Then there have been times when I was nothing and life was stale and unprofitable. "Like a poorly run bakery," my father said, stepping on the joke. My father stepped on jokes all the time. If jokes were grapes, he would have been in the wine business. Instead he was a successful attorney who had started off as an unsuccessful comedy writer. His first break had come in '52, when he was thirty; a cousin's wife lined him up with a job at *Your Show of Shows*, but he got fired after only one *Show* when he pitched a skit about a dog who couldn't see. There was no joke, really, just a blind dog. "He bumps into things," my father said. It may have been something, but it wasn't funny. When he refused to freshen up a Baverhoff skit, he was shown the door. "They didn't just show it to me," he said. "They asked me to walk through it."

I mention my father only to suggest how imprecise a science heredity can be. My father takes credit for my sense of humor, but the facts do not bear him out. On the other hand, by the time my father was my age, he had already steered his marriage past its ten-year mark, sired a daughter and a son, bought a house in a manicured suburb north of the city, made partner at his firm. What I have to show for myself, I show only *to* myself.

Here's the gist of what I mean.

I gave my wife my walking papers but she didn't walk. She skipped and then, when she thought she was out of sight, broke into a trot. It didn't matter, in the end, as we had known each other only two years and the memory of that first night at the casino was humiliatingly fresh in both our minds. The children that we never had still somehow do not respect me; when I dream of them they are beastlike, with teeth that are too large for their mouths and ears red from screaming. I live in an apartment three stories up from the world's loudest hat-and-belt salesman. And while I make a respectable living as a television executive, the nature of the business is such that I could be on top of the world today and crushed beneath its weight tomorrow. Most of the time I am somewhere in the middle.

A note had been sent to all top executives that informed us that by keeping *Chop Circus*, the network had helped its own cause greatly. The show was a prime-time half hour starring Tetsuharu Kawakami, a compact man with a piercing yell who traveled around the country with his trusty sword, Kabutowari, chopping things. Mailboxes, flowerpots, submarine sandwiches—he chopped whatever he saw. At the end of each show, he offered a humorous monologue filled with piquant observations about the lives of the people he had encountered. He had three catchphrases: "Chop Is All," "All is Chop," and "America and Japan Not Very Different: Chop, Chop, Chop." In reality, Kawakami was not Japanese, but rather a Japanese-American comedian named Steve Toyama who had previously played the sidekick in a cop show called *The Copper and the Chinaman*. No one had cared much when he was a Japanese-American playing a Chinese character, and people cared even less when he was a Japanese-American playing a samurai. It was considered progress. We had opened our pockets to Toyama. We had opened our pockets to the show's creators. We had opened our pockets to the production company. Then we had gone around marveling at how open our pockets were. "If we had lost this particular property," the memo said, "it would have been our own necks that would have been chopped." This was followed by a gap in the letter that seemed to be designed for laughter.

"Today's a whistling day," Rose said as I left, and then proceeded to demonstrate. It took all the goodwill I possess toward fellow man not to cashier her on the spot.

The next day, we had moved on from the *Chop Circus* negotiation. That's what happens in the TV business. Everything goes very quickly. "You have Koppelman this morning," Rose sang out. Her face beamed at the thought of my workday. I slipped into my office a few minutes late, drained a bad cup of coffee, and got ready for him.

Koppelman was Morris Koppelman, who revolutionized the comedy/variety genre in the early 1970s by moving away from the dual celebrity host model toward something he liked to call "zingers and

ringers," and he was in the office that morning to pitch
another show. Koppelman started as a young comedy
writer around the same time as my father, and every
time I took a meeting with him—both times, that is—
my father roared mightily upon hearing the name. "So
Morrie's coming in," he said. "Tell them that Leon
Davis says hello. I hope he says, 'Leon Davis the
lawyer?' because then you can say, 'No, Morrie—Leon
Davis the aficionado of blind dogs.'"

It never came to that.

The first time, Koppelman showed up late, with a
twenty-five-year-old girl he insisted was his secretary,
and he took about four minutes to sell the network on
a Civil War comedy that we never ran. The second
time, the girl was even younger. "Still in secretarial
school," he said. Then, after a beat during which no
one dared laugh, he said, "I'm thinking of coming out
of retirement and writing a TV movie about a love
affair between a fedora-wearing crime reporter and a
professor who teaches about the literature of the eigh-
teenth century. They had literature back then, right?
Anyway, it seems like he'd be the hard case and she'd
be the angel, but he's a pretty straight-up guy and she's
a big drinker with man problems. I'll take no fee up
front but I want a big percentage off the back when the
thing gets made." He got his percentage, which was calculated against total revenues of zero. That was his
second strike, and though he seemed calm enough

whenever he'd call in to try to get an appointment, I knew that he was boiling inside. He had two strikes on him, and Morris Koppelman didn't strike out.

So now he was back. He arrived unaccompanied. Maybe his secretary had a math test. "Hi, ho," he said. "Today I'll be serving up the best dish yet. It takes place in space. What doesn't, you may say. I mean that it takes place in outer space. It's the twenty-fifth century, and our hero is a lawman who could have come from the Old West, except that he's not in the Old West." He paused and drew a deep breath. "He's in the Very, Very, Very, Very, Very, Very, Very, Very, Very, Very, Very, Very, Very, Very, Very, Very New West."

Somewhere around the dozenth "Very" a woman had come into the room. We were all listening to Koppelman, or desperately not listening, but she was above the fray. She stood by the door, lousy with elegance. Koppelman finally ran out of breath, and that was her cue to introduce herself. "Mary Grooms," she said. It sounded like a sentence, and a true sentence at that. She had lustrous, long hair and a business suit that had been tailored to within an inch of its life. She looked like a mannequin, except for her eyes, which carried sadness and anger and all the other things her impeccable manners wouldn't permit her to set down.

"I'm assisting Mr. Koppelman on this project," she said.

"Welcome," I said.

She sat to Koppelman's right and folded her hands; he went on about the outer space lawman. "He jets around in a little bullet-shaped car with a fin. He solves crimes and keeps the peace. There are, you see, many space races that have cropped up, and they don't get along. The green-bloods don't like the purple-bloods. The four-noses don't like the two-noses. No one has one nose except the humans. They're just like us. One nose." He was clearly sailing on inspiration. "So there are morality plays, plots that teach us not only who we have become here in the human race, but who we might one day become." He raised a finger as if to make a point but instead he fell silent.

The silence persisted for an uncomfortable duration. Here was where Ms. Grooms came to his aid. "Yes," she said. "There would also be the opportunity to lightly satirize the events of the day by instead setting them in the distant future and imagining how these purportedly sophisticated races resolve their conflicts."

Koppelman's finger was still up; for lack of anything better to do with it, he jammed it into his nose. "Oh, oh, oh, oh, oh," he said. "There's something else I meant to say but didn't. This guy, this rootin', tootin', space-shootin' buckaroo, now and again shows an interest in science. In those episodes, there's no conflict at all, no black-hat, white-hat action. Instead we get soft music, music of wonder, and we show him going off in his bullet car to discover a new planet. Do you know that feeling of discovering a new planet? It's like hiring a new secretary." He licked his lips and leaned toward Ms. Grooms. "Remind me that I have to do that. Must be able to type at least fifteen words a minute and polish the boss's apple at the same time." Here, he laughed at his own joke—or rather, he began to, and then pitched forward onto a wastebasket. His head bounced back up to an alarming altitude, confirming my suspicion that it was made of rubber. I knew that the wastebasket wasn't.

"Well, then," Ms. Grooms said, standing quickly. "Let's call an ambulance and see what we can do about Mr. Koppelman not exactly being dead." The men in the room all scrambled for their phones. There was something in her tone that made you want to scramble.

The paramedics were unable to revive Koppelman and he was pronounced dead on the scene, right beneath a poster of his 1971 variety special *Zip!* I told my father that they were not to blame, that when we had called, they were there in an instant. "Don't you mean that they were there in a heartbeat?" he said. The cataract of laughter that poured from the telephone would have been more appropriate if we had been watching a selection of choice clips from *Your Show of Shows*, or even *Chop Circus.* "I like that," he said when he could catch his breath. "The paramedics were there in a heartbeat. You should use that in something." The memory of his old friend hung between us notionally.

"It is my mission to make good on Morris's dying wish," Ms. Grooms said. We were in the cafeteria. I was nervous around her. Who is not nervous around an elegant woman? I showed her how I could juggle two hard-boiled eggs without breaking either. Usually that was a surefire trick. She saw right through me, though. "I need to focus on how to make things happen. I wonder if you can be of any help."

"What was his wish?" I said. I didn't remember him making a wish. Certainly he had not blown out any candles.

"He wanted the space law show to air on your network. In the last few weeks, it was all he could talk about." Was this part of dying, technically? When he was making his desires known to Ms. Grooms a few weeks earlier, they were merely hobbyhorses. Unless, that is, he had known he was going to die, in which case he would probably have moved the wastebasket. I was still trying to puzzle through it all when Ms. Grooms put the contract on the table. "Sign?"

"This had better be an organ donor agreement," I said. "Anything else, and we're going to need lawyers."

"I like a man with a sense of humor," she said. "Who doesn't? But every once in a while I wish for one who doesn't wear it so conspicuously upon his sleeve."

I called a lawyer, who said he'd be down in a minute. While we waited, I juggled more eggs. This time she had no contempt, only indifference, and even that turned to lighter weather once the contract was signed. To this day I cannot say exactly why I complied so readily. In part it was because the premise of the thing—a lawman flying around in space—tapped into my strong sense of justice. In part it was because I was still in shock from Koppelman's death. In part it was because of Ms. Grooms. As I would learn, things happened fast around her. We signed the contract, she beamed, and I felt such a surge of energy from her smile that I went right back to juggling. "Were you as bad as a Chinese juggler?" my father said on the phone that night. "They're always dropping eggs. That's why they have egg-drop soup."

Preproduction began the next week, and along with it, my relationship with Ms. Grooms. She told me in primly seductive language that as long as the network maintained its commitment to *Untitled Koppelman Project*, she would happily treat me to dinner every Tuesday. The first time we went out, she reminisced about growing up in a privileged Baltimore family, attending swank parties in the city's finest homes. Everything was "chez someone," but the pretention was cut by irony. The second time she let her hair down. The effect was immediate. The third time, after we had been to bed, she rolled over and told me that she felt more comfortable with me than fully half of the men she had ever been with. "But that's not an insult at all," she said hurriedly. "Three of them were real princes. I mean it: their fathers were kings. And then there are all the sweet, tender ones, the lapsed priests, the schoolteachers, the boys of barely appropriate age. On the other side, there are louts. You're better than the louts."

"Who was the worst lout?" I said. I was feeling around for an advantage.

"Funny you should ask," she said. "I was just thinking about him. I was married once, you know, and it didn't work out because of loutishness. My husband was James Reuter."

I frowned. "*The* James Reuter?"

"The one and only," she said.

Reuter was an actor who had started on television, in Westerns, and gone on to films, also in Westerns. He had a funny way of holding his gun. It was impossible to justify.

"We worked with him once on a project, and he was a huge headache," I said. "He yelled at technical staff, came late, wrecked his trailer."

"I'm sorry to hear you say that," Ms. Grooms said through her business suit, which she was putting back on. "I was thinking he'd be perfect for the Space Sheriff."

I laughed. She most decidedly did not. Ms. Grooms, it turned out, was much more of a romantic than she had initially let on. When a tanker spills, oil slowly covers the surface of the sea; in that manner, our weekly dinners became dominated by her long, sad, sometimes luminous tale of her courtship with James Reuter. Just two weeks earlier, she had turned the buttering of bread into an erotic prelude. Now, she barely ate, and I felt like an infidel every time I put my spoon into soup. "James was not an easy man, but he was a man," she said. "He was defined above all else by his enthusiasms. And his temper. And his muscles. The cumulative effect of it all was to help me know that I loved him."

I reached for her hand. She did not stop me but I cannot say that she noticed me either. She went on in her business suit.

"The marriage was a disaster," she said. "If we could have made it work, we would have. Still, he was never out of my heart or mind. That's the only reason I got tangled up in this crazy business with Morris, to help James get back into the spotlight. If it weren't for that, I never would have bothered with Morris. He was kind in his own way but he was, otherwise, the stupidest man I had ever met. I always used to say that if they had left him in a room with one of those block-and-peg puzzles, they would have come back to find the peg gone and Morris moaning and saying, 'My tummy hurts.'"

"I get it," my father said that night on the phone. "Because he would have stupidly eaten the peg."

But I wasn't thinking about that. I was thinking that Ms. Grooms had humiliated herself before one man so that another man would not feel humiliated. A third man's humiliation was an acceptable by-product, even if I was that third man. I understood her better than she knew. Our psychologies turned toward one another.

At this point in a project's development there is often a long phase in irons. The network was having trouble coming to terms with James Reuter, who wanted a salary not exactly commensurate with his talent, his stature in the entertainment community, or, for that matter, his earning power. I was not optimistic. Ms. Grooms sensed my reluctance and it turned her into a different kind of woman. Her hair went back up and she spent much of her time lamenting Morris Koppelman. "Maybe he was the one for me after all," she said. "Sometimes in youth you do not see what later in life would best serve you. And Morris was funny. You could give him that. When someone was bothering him for a payment, he used to say, 'I sent him the money care of the cemetery. It's not his address but it will be by the time he gets the money.'"

"That's not his," I said. "It's Groucho Marx."

"A fool pans for fool's gold," she said cryptically, though it was clear that she was hurt.

I hired James Reuter the very next morning.

Reuter was, despite the reputation that preceded him, a pleasant man. Whatever he had been in his loutish youth, he no longer was. He gave Ms. Grooms a cordial hug and a kiss on the cheek. He had remarried a woman who loved God and perhaps that made all the difference. Ms. Grooms and I sat and watched him work through some of the action scenes in *Untitled Koppelman Project*, and we were nothing short of pleased. He threw a punch and took a punch and was some kind of genius at running toward the bullet-car and jumping into the driver's seat through the driver's side window. We shot several sequences that we intended to use repeatedly, with different backgrounds added in by the special-effects department. There was the Space Sheriff shooting a space gun. There was the Space Sheriff talking on a space phone. There was the Space Sheriff looking out over a to-be-determined space vista.

The first sign of trouble cropped up on the second day, which was the first day that Reuter had a speaking line. The show was mostly hardboiled, so he didn't have much to say, but some rudimentary dialogue was needed to push the thing along. The episode, best as I could tell, concerned a Space Ambassador who was revealed to be a double agent working for the evil Space Syndicate. Close-up on Reuter's face, perturbed, and then cue line: "But then he was a spy, and what could you do about that?"

Reuter just could not get it done. The words were all accounted for, and all in the right order, but no matter how many times he tried, it still sounded like the sentence was a train driving off a cliff. By that I mean that it was both disjointed and too insistently connected and ultimately disastrous. It did not very closely resemble human speech.

"James," the director said. "Let's try it again. Remember, your tone should be somewhere around confused and angry. Confused because he's a spy and you thought he was on your side. Angry for the same reason."

"Got it," Reuter said, but he didn't have any part of it. The words fell out of his mouth again.

The director was a man of the new school and as a result he respected an actor's space and would not dare do anything more aggressive than explain. He turned his patient face toward Reuter and furnished additional explanation. The results were the same, and then they were the same again. It seemed that maybe Reuter was the kind of man who would eat a peg and then roll around on the ground, clutching his stomach.

"Can I show him?" I said. The director held up a

hand to stop me, but I was an executive and I came on through. At the mark, I turned and delivered the line. "But then he was a spy," I said, rushing the first half of the sentence, "and WHAT could you do about THAT?"

"Oh," said Reuter. "Now I see." He did, of a fashion; what we had we could at least save in the sound edit. Ms. Grooms got up on her toes and kissed me. Then she tried to pick me up, right there in the studio. But even this was just a little warmth passing between friends.

Everything was going swimmingly. Reuter got the idea and then, as was often the case, he got an attitude about the idea. He started to send notes to the director and the writers. They were hideous things, his notes, scrawled in a childish hand in the margins of a photocopied script. "More action" was the most common. "More romance," a close second.

One day he was there late, inspecting his own wigs, which tended to be silver but were otherwise understated. "I think this pilot's really going to take off," he said. I made a mental note not to relay the comment to my father. "I'm so happy with what will eventually be the product that I think I'm going to get a little drink."

"Please don't go," Ms. Grooms said. "I'm worried."

He laughed. "What are you worried about? That I'll have too much to drink? Those days are behind me."

"That bad things will happen."

"Isn't somebody else supposed to worry about me now? My wife, for example?"

"I know it's absurd for me to say, but I had a bad dream. I dreamed that you left the studio and that everyone was happy, just like they are now. But when you came back, the studio was empty except for me. I was the only one here. And you couldn't get through the door. You kept banging on it and screaming. It was terrifying."

He saluted her incongruously. "Well, I don't believe in superstition. I'm going to go. I'll be back in the morning."

"Will you at least take him along with you?" She pointed at me.

He shrugged. "Okay by me."

I was accustomed to cheap bars. The one Reuter had picked was an affront to me, in a way; it was in a boutique hotel in a trendily run-down area of town. It had a small secret room behind the main room, and there was a small secret pool back there, too. The place was so chic I thought I saw Steve Toyama in the corner with a pair of young women. I sat on a stool drinking a beer and watching a woman swim laps. She was about my age, which means that she was about the same age as Ms. Grooms, and she had long black hair that fanned out like the tentacles of some sea creature. She got out, dried herself off, and came toward the bar.

"How's the water?" Reuter said.

"Not bad," she said.

This was all the foreplay she required. "I'm staying upstairs. Want to come see my room?"

"Catch you in the morning, Executive Suite," Reuter said, slapping a twenty down on the bar to pay for his drink. At least I had succeeded in keeping him from drinking too much.

The next morning the cop show that used the other side of the studio warehouse was clearing out as we came in. Ms. Grooms was at the doctor's for some kind of routine appointment but Reuter was there, right on time, looking fresh. He might have even had a morning swim. One of the cops approached him and asked him where he had been the night before. Reuter named the bar. "Do you go there often?" the cop said.

"There are nights I've been and nights I haven't been," Reuter said. "Who wants to know?"

"I do," the cop said. "On behalf of the police department."

"You're not a real cop," Reuter said.

"The hell I'm not," the cop said. "Tell it to the dozens of guys who finished ahead of me at the academy." The cop went into his pocket for a picture, which he held up. "Did you have relations with this woman?"

It was the woman with long black hair from the night before. She looked uncertain in the picture. Had she stolen something from Reuter, or claimed that he had stolen something from her? I was glad Ms. Grooms wasn't there.

The cop motioned to me, but then I saw that he was motioning past me, to an officer who was standing in the shadows. "We need to look in your car," they said to Reuter.

Both cops walked us out to the car; one went into the trunk and produced a small towel. When he unwrapped the towel he made a sound that was half surprise, half triumph and brought up a knife. There was blood along the edge of the blade.

"What's that?" I said.

"Unless I'm mistaken, it's that girl's blood. She was found murdered in her hotel room this morning."

Reuter claimed to know nothing about it. He could assume a tone of ignorance with the best of them. When he called his lawyer, you could hear the soothing voice on the other end of the line. "I know the guy," my father said when I told him about the arrest that night on the phone. "Good attorney. Your boy has nothing to worry about."

My father was wrong. Reuter confessed the next day. He had grown angry at the woman when she had questioned the quality of his work, particularly his early Westerns, in which he did all his own stunts, and he had made her stand in the doorway while he recreated the knife-throwing scene from *The Desperado Way*. The knife was a big hunting blade whose presence in the room perplexed the police. "You mean you want to know how it got there?" Reuter said. "I'm telling you how: I went down to my car and got it. I have dozens of knives in there." The one he selected ended up with its tip buried in the woman's throat. Reuter never even knew her name, which was Susan.

Ms. Grooms did not show her devastation but it was evident to me by the way she got right back to work. "We need to rehire someone for the part of Space Sheriff," she said. "Morris would have wanted it to go on."

But we were swimming upstream and we knew it. Three weeks later, the head of the network put an end to *Untitled Koppelman Project* with a short, merciless note. That night, Ms. Grooms asked me to take her to the bar where Reuter had met the woman. Then she asked me to rent a room upstairs.

She downed miniature bottle after miniature bottle of gin and then began to sob face-down on the bed. "I once flew from New York to California to see James," she said. "He was starring in the third *Cowboy Power* film. I spent two days in New York getting myself all prettied up for him and we had a wild night followed by a wild day. I can't believe I will never see him in that light again. I had held out hope, you know. I had held out more than hope."

I went to the bar but there was no gin left for me. I was placed in a position of producing consolation.

"Take off your shirt," I said. Up until then most of what I said had been safe. "Just sit there for a while." She did. "Now put it back on and remember that watching you sitting there with your shirt off ranks as one of the best moments of this or any other day."

My strategy, while brilliant, backfired. Ms. Grooms wouldn't talk to me. She left the network's employ and could not be reached by telephone or mail. It wasn't until the third month, when it was evident she would never resurface, that I fell into despair. And it wasn't until I fell into despair that I began to acquire new shows that I was sure from the first would be blockbuster hits. I bought *Sweet Words From the Sky*, about an angel who masqueraded as a country-music singer. I bought *Crime Squad, Junior*, a cop show whose actors were all under the age of twelve. I bought *C.E.O. Chirpy*, a comedy/drama about a bird whose spirit inhabits the body of a successful but emotionally stunted businesswoman. Early testing was through the roof on all of them. "I think we have three more *Chop Circuses* on our hands," one of the other executives said.

I called my father. I hadn't called him much since James Reuter killed the woman in the bar. I told him about the shows, all of which were being added to the network's prime-time lineup in the fall. "That's my boy," he said. I could hear that he was choked up. "That's my boy."

A year passed, or maybe it was two. *C.E.O. Chirpy* received the best ratings of any new show on any network. I celebrated the way a successful man celebrates: there were women and there were cigars and there were additional payments made by my gracious and thankful employers. Rose was fired for suspicion of stealing and replaced by a young Portugese girl who wanted to move up fast in the business. I kept going to cheap bars, but now I did it with a sense of command. One night, I was in one of those bars when I saw Ms. Grooms. She had cut her hair and looked like a much younger woman, an effect intensified by the fact that she was wearing jeans and a T-shirt instead of her business suit. I waved at her. I was a little drunk. She waved back. As it turned out, she was, too. We began to talk. She had not seen a single episode of *C.E.O. Chirpy*, and I said, "Thank you so much for that," though I was not sure why I said it. We laughed like old friends. She pulled her bar stool closer to mine. We were going to happen and I knew it, and that's why I didn't make a fuss: not when she bit my lip in the taxicab; not when she cursed the driver for stopping at the near corner rather than the far; not when she dropped her keys twice, drunkenly, on the stairs; not when she flopped on the bed and pulled me down on top of her; not when she arched her back and put her hands in my hair and called me, lovingly, James.

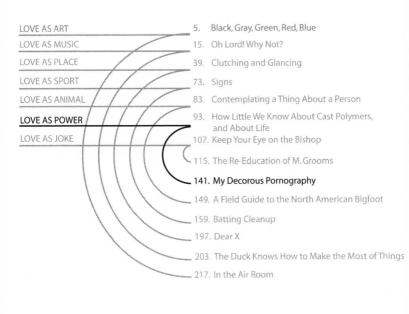

My Decorous Pornography

I want to put my C in Paula's M and my M on her P. I sent her a letter explaining this. She called me when she got the letter and said she was sending it back to me. "Are you angry?" I said.

"Maybe," she said. Then she hung up.

I'm recently widowed, a circumstance that is rare for my age, which is twenty-eight. So rare, in fact, that it's not true. First of all, I think you have to be married to be a widower, and I have just lived with someone for a while. Second of all, that someone has to be dead, and Sarah isn't dead. She's still living and, as a matter of fact, still living with me here in El Paso. We are happy in some ways and unhappy in others. Sometimes we talk through the night. Some days we hardly even talk. This is what passes for life. And even this account isn't true. I'm not in El Paso, but in another

Texas city. The women's names aren't Paula and Sarah, but rather names with the same first letters. I didn't need to do it this way—whether this piece of writing is a memoir or a piece of fiction or something in between, probably the same numbers of people will identify with it and the same numbers of people will be indifferent to it—but taking events that are, in some sense, documentary, and then shifting them a few inches to the right lets me see my own life at a slight remove, where it is more easily endured.

Paula is a friend of mine who is not just a friend. We spend quite a bit of time together, often during the evenings, and I have begun to tilt toward her with a mix of enthusiasm and fear. For much of the time that we have been friends, I have been living with Sarah, which is an obstacle, although not an absolute one. A half-dozen times in the last year, Paula and I have ended up in her apartment, taking off each other's clothes. They're usually botches, these rendezvous. Once I got sleepy because I was drunk. Once I got sloppy. Once she had a sudden fit of pique over the fact that I have a live-in girlfriend. Once she was having her period. Once we had sex, hungrily, and I was finished in a few minutes, half inside my own pants, which was a source of terrible embarrassment for me. And once I couldn't get it up at all. They haven't exactly been Fourth of July celebrations, if you know what I mean. After the last time, which was the time when I couldn't get it up at all, she got dressed in silence and we went to a diner down the street from her apartment. "Maybe we're just supposed to be friends," she said. I nodded because I understood what she meant, not because I agreed. Then I went home and expressed my disagreement by writing her a pornographic letter.

The first letter was the worst one. It was a story about the two of us hopping in her father's pickup truck, driving down into Juárez, and then coupling fervently in an alley off the Avenida. It was very elaborate, with lots of details about the weather and the car, about the clothes she was wearing and how she would wriggle out of them, about the hair in certain places and how it smelled and felt to the touch. There was also an epic metaphor of border-crossing and going south. She hated that letter, and she called me on the phone to tell me so. I sat right down and wrote another letter. "I want to come over and put my C in your M while we are watching TV," I wrote. "Then I want your Ts around my C for a while, and then after you put your M on my C again and I put my M on your P, I'll put my C in your P."

That letter she hated even more. "This is stupid," she said. "I don't even get it."

"You don't understand what the letters stand for?" It occurred to me that maybe she was thinking in Spanish. Her parents are Mexican though her English is perfect.

"*Joder*," she said. "I understand what the letters stand for. But why can't you just write out the words?"

"Because I want you to think about it," I said. "To really think about each of these things as a separate act of pleasure."

"I think about that when I'm doing them. And the question right now is whether or not I want to be doing those things with you. Whether we should be doing them at all."

"Well, I know the answer to that."

"You say that you do, but you're just as unsure as I am. Why else would you write this kind of letter?" Paula is either smarter than I am or dumber, because she often asks these kinds of questions, which I can't answer except by stammering.

"I don't know," I said. "All I know is that this is a letter about what I want to do. If I write that I want to touch your ass, it sounds awkward. I can tell you that in the heat of the moment, but I can't write it down. It seems silly on paper. Too many people write that kind of crappy pornography. Have you looked around on the Internet?"

"No," she said.

"Well, it's everywhere," I said. "I want to touch your A, on the other hand, is something that sounds idiotic now when I'm saying it. But written down, it's kind of nice, don't you think?"

"In a way," she said. "But I'm hanging up now."

"Check your e-mail in a few hours," I said.

"Okay," she said. I didn't send a pornographic e-mail. It didn't seem right. Instead, I sent an e-mail that reminded her that on Thursday we were supposed to go out and see a friend's band. I told her I'd swing by and get her after work, and maybe we could go for drinks before the show.

Then I sat down and wrote another letter. In the letter, I told her that I wanted to touch her A, and to lay my C on it while she was pretending to sleep, and then to touch her Ts and her P while she was on all fours, and then to have her take my C into her M in a pitch-black room. Then we would turn the lights back on and maybe the radio. She would sit on my lap, facing me, so that her P was snug around my C. My hands would be reaching around her, touching her lower back and her A. My M would be on her M. We would be kissing. The letter is sitting there now on the table by the front door. It's folded inside an envelope. Rather than mailing it, I think I'll give it to her when I see her. I'd like to sit next to her while she reads it, thinking about lightly stroking her knee, instead keeping my hands neatly folded on my own.

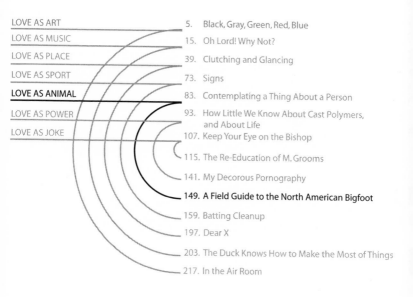

A FIELD GUIDE TO THE
NORTH AMERICAN BIGFOOT

1. Alert.

2. Tired.

3. Thinking of going swimming.

4. Worrying that he is overdrawn.

5. Plotting to avenge himself on his mortal enemy, Alan, who has, over the years, stolen two of Bigfoot's girlfriends, framed Bigfoot for a crime he didn't commit (a minor shoplifting infraction, admittedly, but it's the principle of the thing), and played innumerable pranks that resulted in Bigfoot's humiliation, including one in sophomore year of college in which he dumped an entire pepper shaker into Bigfoot's milk carton and laughed when Bigfoot had to spit out the peppered milk. Alan Tresser. What a jerk.

6. Itchy.

7. Hungry.

8. Enthusiastic.

9. Thinking of Clara—ah! Clara. What a pity that she had nothing to her name and so was forced to factor in wealth when she felt around in her heart for her real emotions concerning this man, or that one. If only her father had given up his dream of sculpting "the intersection of time and tempo," or "the smallest available unit of rhythm," or whatever it was that he was on about in those masses of knotted metal. His sculptures had mathematical names; he had started as a musician and was eternally in search of the Pythagorean comma. "They should all be called 'Bottom of a Bottle,'" Bigfoot said once, unkindly, of Clara's father's sculptures, and instantly regretted it, for her father was a kind man, almost as tall as Bigfoot, though he stooped when he stood, and he did not put his eyes wide and scream like a child that night that Clara brought Bigfoot home. In fact, he was cordial, gave

Bigfoot a firm handshake, let him sit at the table with the rest of them, and the only sign that there was anything amiss came later, when he pulled Clara aside in the hallway and dipped once, quickly, to her ear, where he whispered, "Honey, maybe he's not right for you." In the car on the way back, Bigfoot mocked Clara's father. He could do the voice perfectly; it was light and too sweet, like a bad dinner wine. "Not right for you, not right for you," Bigfoot said, in singsong. That night Clara wouldn't share his bed, and the next week she told Bigfoot that she was seeing a man named Kevin. "He's a lawyer," she said. "You don't know him. But he makes me happy." Bigfoot stepped backward to protect what was left of his dignity. In his heart he experienced a mild pain.

10. Experiencing mild pain.

11. Experiencing moderate pain.

12. Experiencing severe pain.

13. Wondering how much more he can take. First, there was the kid in the shoe department in the sporting goods store who said he'd go downstairs and check the stockroom when he knew full well that there were no shoes big enough to fit Bigfoot's big feet. Then there was the sleek, impossibly thin woman, probably a model, who asked Bigfoot if he knew where she could get a good wax. Bigfoot didn't know what she was talking about. Some days Bigfoot felt like he didn't understand people at all. Then there was the envelope that he found slipped under his door. It was addressed to him, but it had not ended up in his mailbox. This happened a few times a week; the mailman delivered his letters and packages to Mrs. Biedermeyer in 3B. This infuriated Bigfoot. The names weren't even slightly similar, except for the fact that they both started with the same letter. Bigfoot opened the envelope and learned to his horror that

Clara was scheduled to marry Alan Tresser on September 8 in a small ceremony in St. Joseph's Church in the center of town. Bigfoot was invited. This really is the final straw, Bigfoot thought as he went down to the street, got into his car, drove the two hours to the Berkshires, and rampaged in the woods for the better part of the evening. One young hiker scrambled to avoid Bigfoot, slipped on a rock, and got a deep cut on his shin. That should have made Bigfoot feel better, but it didn't. The young hiker wasn't Alan Tresser.

14. Sweaty.

15. Congested.

16. Afraid to reply to the wedding invitation one way

or another. If he did not accept, could he ever hope to speak to Clara again? But if he accepted, that would be a thousand times worse. He would be standing out on the lawn all by himself, or with a date whose name he could not remember from one minute to the next, and he would be making small talk about the bride and groom. "She looked lovely," one old woman would say. "So pink." Bigfoot would not answer, secretly convinced that he should tear off the old woman's head and push the headless corpse down the rolling hill in front of the church where, just moments before, Clara had turned and lifted her chin and, beaming, given herself to Alan Tresser. How had they even met? The last Bigfoot heard, Alan Tresser was working as the regional sales manager for an automotive magazine. Was that enough to give Clara a good life? And what was a good life, anyway? Certainly not one with too much Alan Tresser in it. Bigfoot was sitting at his breakfast table dragging his claw through the dregs of some oatmeal. "I wish I were dead," Bigfoot said to no one in particular. The lifespan of a Bigfoot was three hundred years. Bigfoot had at least eighty to go.

17. Contemplating his death.

18. Dead.

Batting Cleanup

The Orioles got President Clinton, the Braves got Hank Aaron, and at Comiskey, Robin Williams, who was filming a movie in Hyde Park, was preparing to bring down the house with a round of wisecracks and the time-tried fake-windup routine. But the Cubs were on the road, opening against the Mets, and in New York the ceremonial first ball was escorted to the pitcher's mound by a cherub-cheeked boy who smiled shyly and gingerly transferred possession to eighty-three-year-old Annelise Howard Kimball, the only surviving child of New York sportswriting legend James Thurman Howard. "Thank you very much," said Ms. Kimball, her voice scratchy in the loudspeakers. "As Papa loved to say, bring on the heat." And she brought it on, coughing the ball three feet, maybe four, in the general direction of the catcher. The public address announcer gamely bellowed, "Steeeeerike!" The Shea crowd roared. The season had begun.

"Have you ever read J. T. Howard?" Steven asked. He was standing in front of the TV, partially blocking Boyce's view. Anne knelt in the far corner of the room, surveying Steven's bookshelf. Her nail ticked across the spines.

"Sure," Boyce said. "Remember you gave me *Deep to Right*? And I also have that book of essays about the war years, *Fresh New Uniforms*."

"Once he wrote this very equivocal, very lyrical Opening Day column," said Steven, who wrote uncomplicated, hardly lyrical sports columns for a Chicago weekly. "It was from late in his career, the 1948 season I think. I've never seen it in the books, but my father memorized it. Memorized it then, I mean. He was only twelve."

"Are you going to keep it all to yourself?"

"I said my father memorized it, not me. But I know a little bit. Let me see. Okay, I know how it starts. Don't expect Melville, or even Spellman. But it's good for a working newspaperman. Ready?" He cleared his throat theatrically. "'The rapture is in them all, the glazed-over eyes of children, the rolled-up sleeves fresh from the tannery, the dying men whose souls are draining out. And the spring air is rich with the bone of the bat, the blood of the swing, the breath of the ball through time. The practice before the first game is the longest hour on earth. First comes the pitch, then the agony, then the pitch, then the agony. Thunder takes forever. This is not impatience, but love. This is not vanity, but beauty.'"

On the telephone the week before, Boyce had tried, with less grandiloquence, to explain as much to Anne, or at least enough to convince her to accept Steven's invitation. "I don't see how we can not do it," he had said. "He's taking me to the home opener over the weekend, and I think he'd be insulted if we didn't go over there for dinner."

"Do I have to go with you?" she said.

"You don't have to do anything," he said, "but I know he'd love to see you. And I would like you to be there also. It'll only be my second day in town."

"I know. That's why I don't understand why you've committed us to be somewhere. And sports, of all things."

"Anne, it's not just sports. You know Steven's not that naive. Talk to him about painting. Talk to him about symphonies. Talk to him about Freud. He can take it." Finally, Anne had assented, but without any promises of enthusiasm, and soon after they had arrived, she had fallen asleep in a corner of the worn white couch, a biography of Giacometti open beside her.

The Cubs had stumbled to one of the worst records in baseball the year before, and though the new third baseman they had bought from Pittsburgh looked promising, no one was picking them higher than fourth. Never a club to exceed expectations— "poster boys for perennial mediocrity," Steven had called then in his season preview, which forecast a fourth-place finish—the Cubs folded early against the Mets. Trachsel surrendered a run in the first and another in the second, loaded the bases after a two-out error in the third, and then stood and watched like a condemned man as Todd Hundley hit a homer into the teeth of the wind. "Wonderful," said Steven, scribbling notes. "We should wake up Anne. It's rude to sleep at a funeral."

"I'm up," Anne said. "Who's winning?" She rubbed her eyes and ran a hand through her cropped white-blond hair, which was as even and vertical as if someone had planted it.

"The Mets," said Boyce. "By a lot."

"The Cubs will probably open at home without a win," said Steven glumly. "Are you coming to the game Saturday, Anne?"

"No."

"When are you going to come with us to see a game?"

"Never."

"But the Giants will be in for a series the week after next, and then the Braves."

"I don't care."

"It's no use, Steve," Boyce said. "She really doesn't

care. I was in San Francisco with her last summer and she didn't even know where the stadium was. Bury a Rodin in fifty acres of shaving cream and she'll find it, but mention baseball and she goes blank."

"Fifty acres of shaving cream?" said Anne.

"I'm just making a point," said Boyce.

For the two hours and twenty-nine minutes it lasted, the game was torture for the hapless Cubs. A line drive to the shortstop ended up rolling slowly into the outfield, as did a pickoff attempt in which the throw sailed wide of first. The Mets scored their tenth run on a solo shot by Gilkey, and their eleventh on a hanging slider that Olerud cripple-shot over the left-field wall. The TV announcers exhausted "rout" and switched to "shellacking." The fifth Cub who pitched, a rookie hopeful, tore his rotator cuff delivering a slider that was ripped to the wall for a double.

"Cub luck," Boyce mused. A black rubber plug in Steven's phone had come loose, and he was absorbed in the difficulty of extracting it from the depths of the armchair.

"This game is so sad," said Steven. Anne was asleep again, only ten pages more familiar with Giacometti. "Sadder than Cheever. But that's why I love it."

The same could be said for Boyce's relationship with Anne. When you haven't been paying attention to how much freedom you have, sometimes it comes as a shock. His January bank balance, thirteen thousand dollars to burn, not including the three thousand in bonds that lay fattening in a bank in Baltimore, was the key to the whole tinderbox. He had decided to quit his reporting job and move to Chicago, where he could live with Anne and work on his fiction. Anne took to his plan enthusiastically. But he knew it wouldn't be easy to move in with someone, no matter how often he tried to set his mind at ease, no matter how often she did. She would have habits. He would have needs. Things would take time. He reminded himself of this repeatedly on the flight, as if the admission of certain collision would armor him against the impact.

Chicago was a huge brain, dense, gray, and powerful. Boyce had never been there before, but he felt as if he had, largely from his family's stories about a crazy relation who had bolted from Baltimore in 1926 to find his fortune in the Windy City. The young newspaperman had spent the train ride memorizing the downtown streets and the players on both ball clubs—Gabby Hartnett, Charlie Grimm, Sloppy Thurston, Bibb Falk, Pid Purdy—and with the names still swimming in his head, he patched together a new identity for himself. He would conquer the city not as Ray Divitsky, but with the decidedly less ethnic (if comically front-loaded) moniker of Robinson Day. When Robinson's letters back to Baltimore began to report some success as a man-about-town and, as incredible

as it must have seemed, as a poet, Boyce's grandfather
Herman—then an eighteen-year-old auto mechanic
starstruck by his glamorous city-mouse brother—had
become Herman Day in homage. And when Robinson
Day died drunk ten years later in a condemned West
Side apartment, his poetry forgotten and his output
reduced to hack feature-writing, Herman, who was
more sentimental at twenty-eight than he had been at
eighteen and would continue in that mawkish direction his entire life, not only kept the name Day but also
added the middle name Robinson, and made a special
trip west each year to put flowers on his black sheep
brother's gravestone. Boyce's own middle name was
Pentz, after his mother's haberdasher father, and no
matter what his fate in Chicago, he had no smitten
brother to pay him tribute, only his kind, diffident
sister, who was still in high school in Maryland,
studying science and dreaming of doctorhood. He had
recited this history breathlessly to Anne in a phone call
the night before he arrived, shoehorning in a brief
soliloquy about his final week of work and his plans
for his first story, which would tell the tale of a quietly
psychotic man dying as the millennium dwindled. "Is
there any way you can call me back late tonight?" she
had asked. "I hate to be rude, but I have to get out to
the studio to do some work, especially since I have to
take off the next few days."

"No," he said, making no effort to conceal either

his hurt or his guilt over that hurt. "No problem. Of course. I understand. I'll see you when I get in."

Anne's apartment was a fourth-floor studio in a quiet, leafy neighborhood. "It's only twenty-five minutes to downtown by bus," she said, "and I have a great supermarket just around the corner." Inside, the place was cluttered but spirited, exactly the way Anne's apartments always had been, with pages ripped from art magazines mounted on the walls alongside handwritten notes and enlarged, xeroxed fragments from favorite books. One of her paintings, a nude woman in a bathtub viewed from above, sat on the mantelpiece.

"Take a look at the presents I brought you," Boyce said. With a randy laugh, Anne reached for his belt. "No," he said. "In the bag." His voice emerged pinched and shrill.

"Sorry," she said. "I guess I jumped the gun. At the gun, actually." So they sat on the bed, Boyce with his unanswered questions and Anne with her antic eyes, and they opened the gifts: a bottle of burgundy, a pair of hand-carved ivory earrings, and a black silk scarf from Florence.

That first afternoon, they did not make love, just lay sideways on the bed, legs locked like the opposing blades of a scissors. "This reminds me of an Ernst painting of two birds I once saw," Anne whispered. "It was in the National Gallery in Washington. They were kissing one another at the tips of the beaks." Boyce and

Anne fell asleep breathing shallow welcomes into each other's mouths, and when the alarm clock jangled half past seven, they felt lighthearted and content. They ate dinner in a Swedish café ("Making the exotic as bland as possible," he had joked) and rode the bus to the warehouse-like Et Gallery, where Anne's friends and rivals passed before Boyce in such quick succession that he later remembered nothing. While Boyce chatted amiably with a slender brunette printmaker, Anne, her eyes going liquid with the complimentary rosé, argued with a small man in a brown corduroy cap over Alex Katz. "His work," she said, "began with a flourish but ended in midboast. If his works were cars, they'd rust out. If they were birds, they'd fall out of the sky." The man listened with a messy smile, stirring his wine with an index finger. From his vantage—he was standing inconspicuously in the shadow of a sheet-metal elephant—Boyce marveled at her. She wore her red dress like a fire. He explained this to her on the way home. The wine had gone to his head. "Mine, too," she said, as she unbuttoned his shirt in the elevator. Her dress was up around her waist while they were still in the hall.

Some women's contours direct you to their eyes, others to their shoulders and sloping backs, others still to the wide parentheses of their hips and the unspoken phrase contained within. Anne's rather angular features led outward, to her arms, and finally to her hands. The idea of her painting, this fascinated Boyce. He could not connect the short, solid girl beneath him—breasts large and low, pubic hair that crowded her crotch like golden filings massing round a magnet—with the majestic canvases that hung in her studio. Heavyset businessmen clutching cigarette lighters in pathological fists. Demure children absently, innocently, skimming uninitiated fingertips over their own smooth bodies. "All these people are inside me," she had told the small man at the opening, by way of explaining that while she painted from photographs, the works were not portraits, and in addition to finding the depth of her conviction admirable, Boyce had experienced a strange twinge of sexual jealousy, as though the man sitting on the bed or the girl lost in a swirl of vague green intended to box him out, to keep him from her bed. But as wistful as he felt beside her that night, deaf to whatever ghosts animated her hands, it was nothing compared to the emptiness of idly sitting around her apartment the next day, making indentations in the pile rug with the end of a Budweiser can, rereading the comics time and again as if intense scrutiny might reveal a fantastically satisfying subtext, turning on the television from boredom and turning it off minutes later from for the same reason. He had started to scribble preliminary notes in a sketchbook Anne had loaned him, but after ten minutes he couldn't concentrate. His idea for the story seemed thin. He switched to another idea, one about a circus clown who loves a woman in the acrobatics troupe but despairs that she won't take him seriously as a suitor. "Just be patient," he said aloud. Things took time.

At seven in the morning, Boyce was up in bed reading the *Tribune* when Anne startled him by shooting upright, clutching his arm just above the elbow as if they were promenading, and shouting, "My nose hurts." She woke again at eight with no memory of the earlier incident. But her face was puffy and her head "absolutely splitting," and no amount of obeisance on his part could lift her spirits. In bed, she complained that she needed to pay her bills. In the kitchen, she lamented the apartment's disarray. En route to the shower, she caught her shin on the edge of the bed and cursed half-heartedly. Boyce lay flat on his back with his eyes shut.

Then, the hot floral fumes of her emerging from the shower. Then, the soft clicks as she dialed the phone. "Hi, Mother, it's Anne. Good. And how are you and Dad? Things are fine, except that my apartment is a mess, which is fine in its own way. How's Lighthouse? Is the swelling in his eyes gone? You can send him out to recuperate with me if you'd like. I could always use a helpful pair of paws around the house. Yes, I did get the photos. The baby is adorable, isn't she? But Susan looks so tired and worn. I feel like an absentee aunt. I got some work into a student show in the middle of the week. No, nothing else much. The apartment is so dirty. So anyway, Mother, I should get going. Yes, he's here. He's fine. I'll tell him you said hello. For about two weeks. So far, so good. I go to my studio all day and he stays at home and writes. We're eating at his aunt's next week. Okay. I'll talk to you soon. Good-bye."

Anne's conversations with her parents had always been polite, even professional, in a way that was entirely alien to Boyce, who steeled himself for a full fifteen rounds every time he called home. He was sure the cheery lilt in her voice had been an act for San Francisco, but now, as she brown-bagged her banana-and-yogurt lunch, she seemed perfectly content. Where had the anger gone? Had it just blown out the window? Had it swirled down the shower drain? Had Anne tossed it out with her coffee grounds?

"I told my mom we were going to your aunt's. She asked if I was going to dye my hair black and pretend I was Jewish."

"There are blond Jews, you know," he snapped. So that's where the anger had gone.

"I know, but they're not as common."

"Oh, so you want to be a common Jew. In that case maybe you should get big calluses on your hands and fingers and smear chicken fat on your face and neck."

"I'm sorry. I didn't mean anything by it. There's certainly no terrible connotation associated with black hair. But tell me, how should I behave at your aunt's?"

"The same way you would anywhere else, except try to keep the Holocaust jokes to a minimum."

"That is the way I would behave anywhere else. What kind of jokes can you make about the Holocaust?"

"How about the one about Hitler and the farmer's daughter?"

"I'm afraid I don't know it."

"Hitler was out riding in his Mercedes convertible with some friends when he spied a young farm girl. Despite his single undescended testicle, he felt himself aroused. 'I must have her for just one night,' he told Goebbels, who was sitting in the back seat next to him. Are you listening?"

"Unfortunately."

"So anyway, he decides he's going to make a play for this farm girl. He writes a letter to her father on very official Third Reich stationery, cream white paper with dove white trim, sealed with a swastika. The letter begins, 'Dear Citizen: I would like to request an audience with your daughter.' The father desperately wants to impress Hitler—who wouldn't?—so he orders her to go. The night before she is to be driven into Berlin, she sleeps fitfully, wondering if Hitler will marry her and make her empress of the Reich. You know, those Bavarian farmfrau fantasies. The limousine that comes for her is upholstered in leather, with fur trim on the headrests. At the Reichstag, Hitler greets her at the door, kisses her hand, and the two of them feast on duck prepared by the finest chefs of Germany. After dinner, Hitler leads her into a courtyard. In it are two huge stones. Chained to one stone is a huge naked man with rippling muscles and smoldering eyes. He's as big as Samson, as beautiful as Apollo. Chained to the other stone is a mangy dog. 'Here, my dear girl, we have an exercise,' says Hitler. 'Which of these two beasts do you find more appealing?' The girl looks at the dog, at the mattery sores and bare patches on its legs, at the rib cage visible through the skin. The stench of the cur almost overwhelms her. Then she looks at the man, who is striking, and she looks him up and down until she sees that his penis is—what else?—circumcised. 'Herr Hitler,' she says, the pride filling her voice, 'I would choose the dog.' 'Great,' says Hitler, loosening his belt. 'So I get to fuck the Jew again!'"

"That's horrible," said Anne.

"Thank you," said Boyce.

"Hitler wasn't gay, was he?" said Anne.

"Is that the point of the joke?"

"No," she said. "I understand the point of the joke. I'm trying to change the subject."

"No. I don't think he was gay. But he was a coprophage."

"What's that?"

"A shit-eater. It gave him great sexual pleasure."

"Disgusting." Anne's mouth turned down at the corners.

"As if you'd expect decorum from a genocidal tyrant, or at worst, eating the entrée with the salad fork. Did you ever read that self-help manual, *Mein Kampf*?"

Anne—intent on reading the newspaper, or on ignoring Boyce—refused to answer. Boyce didn't know why he was coming down on Anne so hard. His parents, who lit Shabbat candles once or twice a month, conducted a Passover seder in patchy Hebrew, and scoured the *Times* every day for news of Israel, were about as observant as the family got. His grandparents' generation had been too busy keeping businesses afloat to bother with the inconvenience of religion; old Ray Divitsky, as far as Boyce knew, had never even set his assimilated spats inside a synagogue. And Anne, who pounced righteously upon even the most benignly impolitic generalizations—except, of course, those voiced by her own mother, who was a volunteer nurse in San Francisco and should have known better—was certainly no bigot. "Anne," he said, trying to keep his tone even. "Have you read anything about that play *Don't Send Nobody Nobody Sent*? It's about politics in Chicago under the Daley machine. Steven really wants to go see it. I told him we couldn't go Wednesday, but maybe Thursday."

"I have to be in the studio until ten."

"I know," he said. "We can go to a late performance then."

"I'll be tired. The two of you should go without me."

"No," Boyce said. "I want you to come. We'll wait until the weekend, or whenever. We'll advance-order tickets for whatever night you want."

"I don't know if I can go on the weekend."

"You're working on the weekend? How much can one woman paint?"

"I need to keep a schedule. It's very hard to make things. It requires tremendous discipline."

"So you're going to deny yourself all pleasures."

"Painting is my pleasure. I like going to the theater, but I don't need any more. And I don't like the feeling that we have to argue about these things all the time. Since you got here, you haven't stopped talking a mile a minute about the things we'll do. Dinners. Concerts. Even baseball games, for god's sake."

"You don't like doing things with me?"

"I don't like feeling that you need to be entertained all the time."

"That's me, supervision from dawn 'til dusk, and lots of pretty colors and noises. Day care. I wasn't aware your creative life was worth so much more than mine. I wasn't aware that I needed to know some sort of higher math to see how many of my writing minutes make up one of your painting minutes, or that wanting to spend a night out with you turned me into some sort of spiritual welfare dependent." But of course her time was more valuable—whose time is worth less than the man who cannot act except to beat down the woman who can?—and she proved it by tersely, decisively, presenting him with the flat of her palm.

"Let's drop it."

After Anne had left for the day, Boyce sat down at the desk with a hot cup of tea and tried to re-create the morning's conversation. He thought he might use it, or a version of it, in his story—the clown had finally worked up the courage to speak to the beautiful acrobat, and she had rebuffed him with a laugh. She didn't have the time for him. But in attempting a transcription, he grew even more confused. It seemed as if he had overreacted at every possible turn, wrenched the wheel left or right when a gentle turn would not only have sufficed, but also have spared the equipment unnecessary wear. Even when Anne had kissed him a gentle good-bye and issued what seemed not only a sincere apology but an honest attempt at understanding the tension—"I'm sorry about our fight. I worry about it the same way you do. I give so much to my painting, and it never seems to be enough. I'll make more time for the two of us"—he had drawn his bow and let fly a look that was tipped with malice, and the fact that it was delivered in half-jest couldn't eclipse the half that was serious. The more he tried to keep an even surface to his tone, the more the corners of the carpet lifted and ugly things crawled out.

What to do? What to do? Anne had mentioned to her mother that the apartment was dirty, and it certainly was. Maybe his internal disarray had something to do with that. Anne spent all day in her studio, not by any means impeccable but at least suited to her needs, but his daily haunt was this apartment—an ugly hybrid of her bad habits and his, hard to work in, if not impossible. He had felt it most acutely the day before, when he had gone to the medicine cabinet for aspirin, and couldn't find any among the scattered scraps, leavings, and fragments of various personal hygiene products. He had finally found the bottle, cap doffed, on a gummy soap shelf to the right of the sink, but by that time his headache had grown to daunting proportions, and he could no more return to his writing than he could hoist the world onto his shoulders. He had gone for a walk to clear his head and ended up in the Wrigley bleachers, watching the last four innings of a lackluster Cubs victory over the Phillies. Today, though, his strength was replenished, and he was determined to make progress—if he couldn't absolutely finish, he could at least get most of it done. First, he moved all the items onto the top of the toilet tank; then, he started to move them back into the cabinet one by one. The uppermost of the three partitions, short and shallow, was best suited for cosmetics items (L'Oreal Mattique, lipsticks, eyebrow pencils) and long, narrow tubes of ointment and lubricant (CortAid, benzoyl peroxide, K-Y Jelly). The middle shelf shouldered the meat of the cabinet's contents—from left to right, toothpaste, deodorant, first aid, hair care, lotions, and soaps. And on the bottom went the miscellaneous items: shaving supplies, condoms, perfumes, and prescription medications. Occasionally, size required the violation of these thematic groupings: a small jar of humectant pomade, which looked out of place in the haircare section, fit neatly alongside a half-moon bottle of Simoom. The only item his system could not accommodate was a box of tampons, a package of twenty-seven with only eight remaining. Should he discard the paper box and stack the individual tampons in the cabinet? He decided against it, and threw away a pair of plastic safety razors to make room.

With the purifying thrill still with him—the sight of his reflection in the cabinet's mirrored door was immensely more satisfying now that he knew that a world of rational order lay behind it—Boyce moved from the medicine cabinet directly to the desk. That was the wonderful thing about organization, that you could apply the same strategies to different sets of data. The rules were logical and almost irresistible. All you had to do was repeat until satisfied.

Anne's frustrating disregard for shaping space—a painter, Boyce reflected, should understand—was especially evident in her desk, or rather the top two drawers of her desk, which housed her collection of cassettes. Most of them were presents from Boyce from their time in Durham, where he hadn't lived with her but had been a regular visitor to her apartment. He had asked her once how she arranged her tapes. "The ones on the top are the ones I like; the ones I don't like are on the bottom." He didn't have the heart to tell her that even her explanation was disorganized, that the two halves of the sentence weren't parallel. Here, things were no better. Sam Cooke was sprawled atop a jumble of Styx-and-Stones seventies rock, which in turn buried Otis Redding and Solomon Burke. The Byrds' *Sweetheart of the Rodeo*, boxed in by Ohio Players and Earth, Wind & Fire, could hardly see clear to Gram Parsons's *Grievous Angel*. And in an inadvertent pun, Carole King adjoined Queen instead of Laura Nyro. *Tapestry*, indeed—more like *Travesty*. The shallower of the drawers held twenty-two cassettes in each of four rows; the deeper, two levels of three rows of fifteen cassettes each. Boyce sorted the entire set into rock and pop, funk, blues, soul, and jazz; subindexed alphabetically by artist; and organized each artist's works chronologically. Only one cassette confounded his blueprint, a tape that had Tim

Buckley's *Greetings From L.A.* on one side and the daunting "Mozart Mass in C Minor K 427 Kyr: Battista Pergolesi Stabat Mater" (lettered in a hand he didn't recognize) on the other. Boyce hated classical music; though it was the very model of organization, it seemed to be the work of men who thought they understood it all. While he was debating whether to inaccurately file the cassette under Buckley or simply erase the Mozart and replace it with *Sefronia*, the phone rang. It was a friend of Anne's, a painter named Diane. "Could you tell her I called?" she said.

"Can and will," said Boyce.

With the split mix sequestered in his pocket while he pondered its fate, Boyce opened the window, first removing the ivory earrings from the sill where Anne had carelessly left them. A recent rain had fallen on the nearby rooftops and made the tepid wind smell of tar. On a screened balcony, a woman held up a watering can in a way that reminded him of his mother. He couldn't tell how many streets away the building was. The horizontal grid of blocks and streets and the vertical staff of fire escapes and windows that rose before him were two different systems that seemed never to harmonize. Not with each other, not with him.

On Sundays, Anne liked to read the *Tribune* perfunctorily and then luxuriate in the *Times*. On his way to buy the paper, Boyce whistled a Sam Cooke song,

"Meet Me at Mary's Place." It had been more than a week since he had cleaned out the tape drawer, but every morning since then he had woken up with a new memento of the experience rattling in his head. They stayed with him while he showered, while he shaved, while he ate breakfast. He told himself that he should expect a little backup in the system, but to have these trifles—"Rock and Roll Band" on Tuesday, "Your Number of Your Name" on Thursday, and the cruel irony of "Tears of a Clown" as he stared forlornly at his stalled story on Friday—come up on him with such vehemence, to regularly regurgitate undigested chunks of other people's work, that was worse than inconvenient. That was humiliating.

Unable to work but unwilling to be depressed in a city so new, Boyce had been accompanying Steven to Wrigley on a regular basis. After leaving the game, they would retire to a small sandwich shop on Clark—named Lobster Pizza, after the house specialty—and talk through the day's action. A number of one-liners Boyce had composed during those sessions had appeared in Steven's column: "Two-Card Studs" when a pair of St. Louis pitchers combined to one-hit the Cubbies; "Glove means never having to say you're sorry," when the home team downed the visiting Dodgers with three brilliant double plays. Steven had invited Boyce to submit his own columns to the paper—a little competition to keep things interesting—but Boyce didn't think he could. He needed to push ahead with his own work, not hack for pay. And he'd hate to become neutralized by fate.

Anne was sideways in bed, tipped-boat style, blue nightshirt pulled down over her knees, when Boyce let the *Times* drop with a thump onto the mattress. "Paper, ma'am," he said, and got into bed beside her.

"Thank you, paperboy. Could you be so kind as to hold the paper off to the side of the bed until I'm a little less tired?"

"You get two services. You get delivery, and you get paperboy. Removal costs extra."

"Oh, it's you," Anne said sleepily, nuzzling Boyce's stomach with her head. With her foot, she kicked the paper onto the floor.

"Listen," he said. "Can we keep the papers off the floor? I made a pile for them over there."

"Okay, I'm sorry." She giggled. "Old woman."

"Is there a problem with keeping things organized?"

"They are organized."

"For you, maybe. But why not do it in a way that makes sense to more than one person?"

"Well, sire," she said. "I appreciate your concern. But let me take this time to ask you about the bathroom cabinet. If you look at how it was organized before, the things on the top shelf were there mainly because I didn't need to get to them. I can't reach that shelf. So now all my makeup is up there. How does that make sense?"

"So you think my system is a bad one?"

"Horrible." She giggled again.

"Stop it," he said. A flush rose into his face. "I take hours and fix things, and all you can do is laugh at me? Before, there was a toothpaste tube cap in the shower from who knows when? November? And shampoo bottles that had been empty for weeks."

Anne turned away in the direction of the line her mouth had become. "I can't believe you're serious about any of this. It just makes me tired. But if you really want to help, you can go in behind that chair in the living room and get all the staples off the floor. My vacuum can't get in there."

"How did the staples get in there in the first place?"

"I staple up drawings in progress. When I rip them out to take them to the studio, the staples fall."

"Okay," he said. "I can do that." Things were beginning to fall into place.

"This afternoon?"

"No," he said. "We're going to a baseball game. Remember?"

"I'm not going," she said. "I already told you. I am never going."

"Why not?"

"Because I have no interest."

"Because you think it's worthless?"

"Isn't it?"

"Hardly. There's so much strategy."

"What? Hit the ball? Hit the ball harder?"

"No. There's everything. Hitters pay attention to pitchers. Pitchers to hitters. There's beauty and grace and drama. It's like theater, but without any predictability."

"I really have to work today."

"How will you learn anything if you don't try anything?" he said. "Are you trying to set a record for being cramped and narrowminded?" Hit the ball, hit the ball harder. Anne's eyes swam with tears. Boyce stroked her hair while he apologized, two vertical strokes and then two horizontal. "I'm sorry, Anne. Really. I don't know why I'm acting this way. It's been harder for me than I thought to come here, in part because it seems so hard for you. And that makes it bad for my energy and my work." Boyce felt dishonest about using the words "energy" and "work." They seemed to have no place in his life. "When I can't work, I don't like to talk about it, and this anger comes from the middle of nowhere."

"Don't you mean 'from left field'?" Anne said.

Boyce shielded his eyes against the sun and watched Cordova mow down another Cub. Only five innings had passed, and already six strikeouts. One for every run the Pirates had scored against Telemaco. "It's as bright as an evangelist's teeth out here today."

"I can't pay you for these, you know," Steven said.

"Your company is payment enough."

"Thank you. You're very insincere. Is it my imagination, or have you refused to answer me every time I've asked about your writing?"

"It's not going well, if that's what you want to know."

"Why not?"

"Can't concentrate, mostly. Why do you think I've been out here at every home game. I'm not filling in a bingo card."

"Weak-ass shit," said Steven, shaking his head.

"What are you, my pitching coach? I think the sports metaphors are going to your head."

"I just think you should stop slacking. You're brilliant. Everyone says so, so it must be true. But there are always these incredibly complicated, incredibly neurotic excuses."

"I wish they were only excuses. It seems like a permanent problem. Maybe I made a mistake in coming here. At the newspaper I rarely had time to write my fiction, but at least I was writing every day. So then I decide I'm too good for it and quit, and what happens? I waste the entire day doing nothing, and when Anne gets home I lash out at her with tirades composed of all the brilliant, Byzantine sentence I haven't been able to get down on paper. The other day she told me I should tape myself, because at least a short story a day escapes through my mouth."

"So tape yourself."

"I can't. That doesn't make sense. Then I'll get self-conscious and stop doing that. I made up this joke about Hitler, and it was pretty good. It would have worked perfectly if I had given it to some bitter son-of-a-bitch in a story."

"You need to give yourself some downtime. You need to let yourself be relaxed, and not kill yourself every five seconds when you're not producing high art."

"But Anne makes high art every day."

"Boyce, she doesn't. I've been to her studio with you, and I see how much time she wastes. She listens to music. She walks around. She reads magazines. Sometimes she naps. Over the course of a week, she's productive, because she doesn't spend so much time worrying that she's not productive."

"Maybe I should get a job."

"I could get you one. You have newspaper experience, and in terms of talent, you're head and shoulders above anyone else there."

"Are you saying I have dandruff?"

"I'm saying that you should force yourself to write, somehow. What are you working on?"

"Nothing, really."

"What about that story you were telling me about? The one with the clown?"

"It's not working out so well."

"Look," said Steven. "It's not as though you're worried that you're producing bad work. That I could understand. You're telling me that you're producing no work. Until you do, I don't think I should be responsible for any distraction."

"Do you mean?" Boyce said, mock horror in his voice.

"That's right," Steven said. "No more baseball for you, young man."

After an abbreviated stay at Lobster Pizza—after "Cubs bats and pitched balls got a Mexican divorce today," he had no more quips to offer—Boyce shuffled back along Addison to the lake and the apartment. Steven was right, of course. It was all about discipline. And Boyce had Anne to learn from: Never earlier than eleven and often after midnight, he would hear her key scratching at the lock. After a half hour of reading in bed, she would simply dissolve into sleep. There was no melodrama, no angst. Every other night or so she would push her body along the length of Boyce's and pull him toward her. When they made love, she would breathe loudly, quickly, and after she came, she would cradle the back of his head as if it were an egg. It was the same every time. That was what he aspired to: routine that freed energy for creation. But he had an equivocal relationship with respect to routine. A memory came to him. He was in Baltimore, in the seventh grade. Every afternoon, he would come home from school and make himself soup, always tomato and always yanked from the stove burner before it got too hot. Then he would sit down, listen to his favorite records, and sometimes fall asleep. By dinnertime, he was well-rested, and he happily related to his parents what he had learned in school. One afternoon, his sister had a friend over, and the little girl asked Susan if Boyce wanted to play with them. "No," Susan said. "He just drinks soup and listens to music. He's weird." He had felt diminished and ashamed, furious at himself for not designing a more interesting existence and furious at himself for caring so much about how other people judged him. Now, fifteen years later, he felt the same way. His ability to put himself at peace had never evolved, and his fruitless periods of solitude left him even hungrier for contact with others. He promised himself that he would write this all down when he got home. It was important that he didn't forget.

As he jaywalked across the intersection of Addison and Broadway, a book fell out of a passing car.

As a display of his love for the acrobat, the clown penciled her initials on his forehead, but then covered them with white greasepaint. Why bear her brand when he couldn't even bring himself to talk to her a second time? As the clown leaned into a corner of the costume trailer and tried to steel himself for the next miserable session of juggling, honking, and falling down—in short, of clowning—the other performers clustered around the central table. They were naked. It was a long-standing ritual, a way of being free with their bodies, a way of understanding that a costume did not change the essential self but only amplified it. The clown, who did not even like to look at himself in the mirror when he was wearing ordinary clothes, stared glumly at his oversize shoes while his circus-mates chattered and strategized. "What if I bugged out my eyes like I was in pain?" asked the sword swallower, his burly hand resting heavily on the fat lady's thigh. "Yes," said the barebacked rider, a willowy redhead. "That's a wonderful idea. I have been thinking of adding a sequence where the stallion stumbles and rolls—the horse trainer assures me it can be done—and I escape injury by leaping to the lowest trapeze." "I would be honored," said the trapeze artist, giving a deep bow in which she splayed her right hand across the milky skin beneath her breasts. The human can-nonball stood rigid, displaying an almost military obsession with gesture. The clown laughed bitterly. He would never have her.

The door slammed. The clown turned. "Anne, what are you doing home?"

"We had a blackout downtown. I lost power in the studio." She dropped her bag roughly to the floor, threw a newspaper down after it, and slumped into an armchair. "How's your work going?"

"Okay. So what are you going to do this afternoon?"

"I thought I'd stay home."

"Great," he said, slowly enough that he sounded insincere even to himself.

"Unless you don't want me here," she said. "Are you busy? I can take a walk? The weather's nice."

"Whatever," he said. Why didn't he go with her, actually? Fifteen, twenty minutes would refresh him. He was already starting to get a little lost in his work. Why was the clown feeling so bad? He had ventured nothing.

Out on Belmont he saw a sign that said WEEKNIGHT PIZZA BAR, $5.95.

"Look," he said to Anne. "Maybe we should go there sometime." Anne glared at him. "What is wrong now?"

"Nothing. We just don't have the money to keep eating out."

"Keep eating out? Have we ever eaten out?"

"Fuck you," she spat, and broke into the street, where she narrowly missed being flattened by the grill-work of a Mercedes truck. The driver, whom Boyce guessed had seen her tear away from him, glared at Boyce with such hatred that he feared the man might bring the truck up onto the sidewalk.

Boyce caught up with Anne in the lobby of her building and stepped into the elevator behind her. The presence of a third passenger, a fat old woman, kept them civil until they were sitting on the bed, both still short of breath. "If you had told me you wanted to sign a suicide pact, I could have had my lawyer draw up the papers before I arrived," Boyce said acidly. A magnanimous man would have understood that her frustration came from losing a day of work and simply let the matter drop. A less magnanimous man, a species of which he was proving himself a textbook example, understood this but pressed on nonetheless. "If you had been killed, your funeral would have been packed with truckers. They probably would have had the service out on I-75 somewhere."

"Don't joke, please. I'm very angry." She tried to read the newspaper.

"You were almost very dead. Would that have been better?" She didn't answer. "Maybe it would have been," he said. "Maybe in heaven they let you paint all the time."

She turned on him. "You're forever jockeying for position, aren't you? Can you one-up me in this conversation? Sure you can. You're so much better at biting remarks, or making me feel stupid by quoting something from a book that I don't know. Here's one: 'He demonstrated the vain idiocies of an intellect more concerned with the delight of its own gyrations than anything else.' Guess who said that? Boyce, the clown story is turning into the most honest thing you've ever written."

Here Anne screamed, or began to scream, for her outburst did not end in the same breath as it began. The newspaper that was in her hand was suddenly in a thousand scraps, floating down around her like ticker-tape. Boyce could only marvel at her. Even her rage seemed more potent than his could ever be. When her screaming stopped, she stood and walked to the bath-room, and for a moment Boyce feared that the next sound he heard would be a hastily evacuated pillbox (bottom shelf) clattering to the tile. But the sound of water came through the door, and then soft, sobbing hiccups. The section she had torn, Boyce saw, was the local news. He reached for the sports.

"Boyce," she said when she emerged from the bathroom ten minutes later. "Let's not do this any-more." He didn't know whether she meant the rela-tionship or the figuring, and he turned to her slowly. "Let's fuck," she said, settling the matter.

He answered through a sad smile. "Who am I to argue?" She told him she loved him more than any-thing and pressed his face with her fingers. They smelled like paint and turpentine.

Anne left for her studio early in the morning. Boyce sat down and—nothing. He cleaned the closet. He cleaned the kitchen. He wondered how much longer it would be before he'd be able to explain why Formula 409 outperformed Kich-N-Off on tiled surfaces. Pots shorter than one foot on the middle shelf; pots between one foot and nineteen inches on the top shelf; all others under the sink. And his head in the god-damned oven.

Boyce sat down and tried to write. Boyce sat down and—nothing. He made lists of songs he knew with the word "clown" in their titles, and then songs with the word "painting" in them, and then songs with the word "nothing." He typed the sentence "A book fell out of a passing car" and then tried to stare it into ignition. These were wholly unintelligent strategies that he resorted to out of blind panic. Anne was wrong about the clown story. He would finish it today, or tomorrow at the latest.

Formula 409 was a breakthrough, less lather and more liquid. It worked in the spaces between the tiles, where other leading brands couldn't reach. Boyce turned on the television. The Cubs were playing the Marlins. He turned off the sound. Then he rummaged through the tape drawer. He refiled Otis Redding before Smokey Robinson. He withdrew a mix made for Anne in Durham, a collection of old blues songs. He rewound to the start of side two to hear "Night Train Blues" by Mississippi Dranes.

Mississippi Dranes was not on the tape. "When I am making this recording the machine has a red light like a little red eye looking at me," said Anne's voice. "In winter I get lonely. There are a billion dots in my eyes. I'm wondering where they all came from. I hope I don't ever lose my sight. I'm wondering what would happen. I'd have to start it all over again. When I was young, like when I was in college, I was brave. I used to be brave. I was brave then. Now it's too cold here, and everyone I love is too far away, and all I have is my paintings.

"I was thinking of the little girl in the rainbow leotard. I think she should have stayed. I wonder if this fear isn't from knowing more and knowing that everything I've done, someone's done before me. When everyone is vying for attention. I think that some days I cannot use my hands. I don't know why. I've been having the strangest dreams." Boyce listened on. She said his name, and then the name of another man, not his, and then his name again. She sang a few seconds of an old lullaby, and then she breathed so close to the microphone it scared him. With the tape still playing, he sat down to write. She told a story about another girl. The town she lived in was under stress. She said how much she loved him. The name was Boyce, and then it wasn't. He turned the volume higher. He stood and paced the room. Outside, the wind skipped along the tar tops of the roofs.

He unplugged the tape player. It ran on batteries. He set it on a stool, and set the stool against the door. She would upend it when she came in. She would enter like a blowhard, thinking about her paintings of men in suits, or her paintings of firemen. The stool would fall on his legs, onto him on the ground, where he would pretend to be sleeping. The fall would damage the tape player, maybe destroy it. She would come to his aid. The girl in the town touched her own lips. She would forgive him. The television crackled. The Marlins jogged to their positions. Boyce lay down and faced the ceiling.

A hit, and then a double play, and then a hit, and then a steal, and then a walk. Base-runners at the corners. The pitch sailed in. The bat flashed. A shot into shallow left. The runner tagged and went. The left fielder scooped the ball and fired. The gray glint of a staple caught Boyce's eye—perhaps he should tidy up behind the chair, while he had the time—as he lay on the rug, started to like laying on the rug, and watched the Cubs go down to end the fourth.

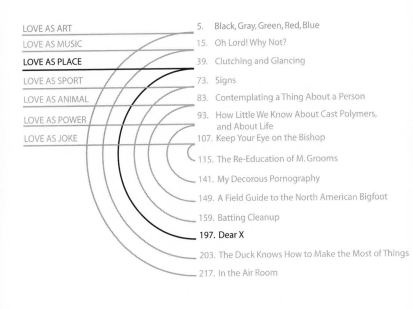

Dear X

Dear X,

I deeply regret the sentiments I meant to conceal, but inadvertently expressed, on our ship-to-shore phone conversation. The roughness of the seas was difficult to detect given the size of the boat. It is, as it claims to be, a "floating hotel," although only the most pernicious abbreviators among us will go so far as to call it a "floatel." The point is that the boat is tremendously large and most waves cannot disrupt its stability. Still, we had a storm and rough weather and I felt it, as a twinge mostly. My stomach was already tender, as I had been gorging myself on the generous portions from the buffet all week—"it's prepaid," my aunt said, "so eat up"—and when the operator connected us I felt a slight drop, as if I were in an elevator that rose an extra floor without warning. Add to that the fact that I had been in possession of a brassiere that you once owned and wore, but that I was in possession of it no longer—a large man with a five o'clock shadow acted the ruffian that first night on the boat, and though I was a gentleman, and bought him drinks, and engaged in the small talk I was taught to devoutly believe would soothe a man like that (I asked after his local sports franchise, after his opinion in cuts of steak, after the difference between one-arm curls and two-arm curls, as far as the growth of the bicep was concerned), he took it upon himself to pound me flat with the hammer of his fist and then to divest me of the afore-mentioned brassiere, which I had kept in my suitcoat pocket like a handkerchief that was too refined for any mortal nose. As for the noses of the immortals, who can say? I am off my line of reasoning. This man strongly resembled Bluto from the Popeye cartoon; he even wore a sailor's shirt, though he did not work on the boat, which was, at any rate, not a sailboat. My sorrow over the loss of that brassiere conspired with the soreness I suffered at the hands of that Bluto; what had settled in me regarding my feelings for you, and your refusal to reciprocate except in the most the-atrical and obvious manner imaginable—not, as I would have liked, in the harum-scarum fashion that would have revealed actual emotions—was stirred again by the effect of the sea upon the buffet. Lunch came up, a bit, and so I came to call you out for what

I felt you were not allowing yourself to feel. It was only at the conclusion of a rather passionate six-minute monologue that I noticed that the phone was upside down, that I had in effect been talking into my own ear. I turned it around and explained that the story was, in effect, metaphor, with Bluto standing in for my feelings for you, the seas for my fears regarding those feelings, my aunt for my feelings regarding those fears, the ship for your eyes (they are lovely green things and the brows over them lovely dark), and the brassiere for your breasts. I told you that I could not take this metaphor in hand. I worried if I ever would, and the very thought made the rest of lunch come up.

Yrs,

  X

The Duck Knows How to Make the Most of Things

The Duck Knows How to Make the Most of Things. That's the name of his stage show, so it must be true.

"Sometimes I cry when I'm lonely," he sings, and the little ducks sing backup, doo-wop, ah-ah-ah-ha-ah-ah. "Sometimes I laugh when I'm blue." Ah-ha-ah-ah-ha-ah. He didn't write the song. It is one of the few in his show, *The Duck Knows How to Make the Most of Things*, that he didn't write. But he sings it like he sings them all.

He's not an actual duck. That would be something, wouldn't it? A duck can't sing, let alone make the most of things. No, the Duck is a man, a rather large man at that, and the little ducks are his children. They are not his actual children. They are students who are enrolled in his music school, the Gifford E. Tannhauser Academy of Vocal Performance. Gifford E.

Tannhauser is his actual name.

The Duck's not married. He was, once, and after years of regret and recrimination his wife finally picked up and went elsewhere. "Two years, to be exact," he says with a twinkle in his eye. This pained him tremendously, but that pain was mitigated by the fact that she moved only five minutes away. They're on good terms, the Duck and the former Mrs. Tannhauser. They have no actual children. They have dinner together once a week at least, just like when they lived together, and the Duck and the former Mrs. Tannhauser throw elbows at one another. "Getting a spare tire, Gifford," she says, pointing at his stomach. She's the only one who calls him Gifford.

"Getting a flat, former Mrs. Tannhauser," he says, pointing at her breasts. "Age is doing us both in. Remember when we were in our prime?"

"Of course I do," she says. "We were flippin' miserable." This always gets a laugh.

The former Mrs. Tannhauser has not remarried. She tells the Duck that she is done with men except for the occasional roll. "I'll tumble but I won't fall," she says. "Isn't there a song like that?"

"Yes ma'am," the Duck says. It is one of the mainstays of *The Duck Knows How to Make the Most of Things*. He begins to sing. "I will tumble but I will not fall / I may crumble but I will not crawl / There are things I'll do for you and things I can't abide / I can't go on forever but I want it said I tried." He gives a bravura performance, tugging on each line of the verse and swelling magnificently for the chorus: "Let's go to the store / I'll buy one, then buy more / Follow my lead / You know what I need / Close the door."

The former Mrs. Tannhauser applauds. "It's not a very good song, is it?" she says.

The Duck turns his palms up in surrender. "Not at all."

The Duck befriended a woman while he was still married to the former Mrs. Tannhauser. This woman's name was June ("like the month") but she preferred to be called J. "Like the letter," the Duck said.

J didn't have an answer for this. The Duck thought she was insulted or, worse, indifferent, but he has since learned that she will sometimes sink into moods where, even though she is experiencing satisfaction or elation, she will not, or cannot, respond to him. Of course, he has also seen her exhibit the same behavior when she feels insulted or indifferent. He once mentioned in passing that he had written a song about her. He thought it would make her happy but instead it made her miserable. "I don't want to be in someone else's song," she said. "I can't bear it."

Many of these moods occurred during the first months of the Duck's friendship with J. "You know what I mean?" he said. "What can I do?"

"You can shut the fuck up." She saw the hurt in his eyes. "You know what? There is something you can do. You can sing me a song or two, softly."

That got him going. He sang "Somewhere Safe to Bury My Bone." He sang "Water Lace." He sang "I Got Big and Fat in a Coldwater Flat." There were more songs in *The Duck Knows How to Make the Most of Things*, but those were the ones he sang.

The singing always worked. One song would bring the first tear and more would follow: more songs and more tears. "The Satisfaction and Elation Flowed out of Her (Saltily)" was the name of the song that the Duck ended up writing about the effect of the other songs.

The crying sometimes took a while.

After J finished crying, the Duck stopped singing and the two of them went for a walk. At first, the walks were just walks, but they evolved over time into something else. They adjourned to a nearby playground and commenced to romp in a decidedly adult manner. The playground was the safest place for miles around. There were guards to keep out the drug dealers and stick-up kids. The Duck knew one of the guards, Alberto. He was once one of the little ducks. When the Duck told Alberto to take a walk, Alberto took a walk, and the Duck and J had their pick: the slides, the swings, the climbing bars.

One day J goes off somewhere and comes back with her hair disarranged. He does not ask her questions because he does not believe in jumping to conclusions. The next day she goes off in the other direction and comes back with her hair disarranged and one earring missing. He does not ask her questions because he believes in giving her a chance to come clean. The next day she goes off in an entirely new direction and comes back with the Bootblack in tow. He does not ask her questions because now it is too late.

The Bootblack is a young man. When he was born the Duck was already teaching a flock of little ducks to sing "Mainsail on the Adriatic," an extremely simple chantey that he wrote as an exercise during his first year as a songwriter. The Bootblack has never sailed. He has never seen the ocean. He lives in a city a few hours to the north, where he has a television show, which makes sense given that he is significantly more handsome than the Duck. The Bootblack is a man of many talents, but one in particular has preceded him: he can swallow a handful of change and bring up specific amounts on command. "Thirty-seven cents," a guest on his show might say, and he will grimace slightly and produce it in descending order: quarter, dime, penny, penny. Sometimes, if he's in a playful mood, he'll follow the quarter directly with a penny, and the studio audience will begin to boo. Then he socks it to them: penny, penny, penny, penny, penny, and so forth, one after the other in quick coppery succession. He'll make them flip end to end on his tongue to give the appearance that they're walking out onto the black mat he has spread before him for his performance. There are many men who can bring up change on command, but this is his move and the one that has made him famous. It's called "pennying." Lined up the way they are, the pennies look, the Duck thinks, like ducklings.

J met the Bootblack at a hotel. She had met him once before, through a friend, and at that time the two of them had not gotten along. They had argued about the distance from the moon to the sun. The Bootblack said that it was a very short distance, and J insisted, correctly, that he was thinking of the distance from the moon to the Earth. The sun was as far away from both as a…she could not think of a way to express herself with clarity and force. "It's far," she told him and told the Duck later, when she was relating the story. In the retelling she was incensed. Her nightshirt was unbuttoned and the Duck was beginning to make the most of it. Her anger gave a slight flush to her face and the skin on her chest and the Duck was grateful to this Bootblack, this nickel-vomiter, this astronomical idiot, for greasing the rails a little bit.

It was the last time he felt that way about him. One day the Bootblack was just a guy you saw when you were flipping from porn to the weather channel, a guy who warmed your friend up inadvertently, and the next day he was sitting next to her in the car as she pulled into the driveway, her hair disarranged. The transformation was so quick that the music that played behind it when the Duck remembered how things had gone was melodramatic soundtrack music, without any vocals. There was no place in it for him to sing. It could not have been included in *The Duck Knows How to Make the Most of Things.*

J skips to the door. Skips! She greets the Duck with a hug and introduces the Bootblack. It is too far for him to drive home, J says, and she tells the Duck that the Bootblack will be eating dinner with them. "It's my night to eat with the former Mrs. Tannhauser," the Duck says. "We're having chicken."

"Wonderful," J says. "We can all four eat."

It is the worst meal of the Duck's life, with the possible exception of the Indigestibly Dry Turkey Incident of '77, which was served up by a very young, very optimistic former Mrs. Tannhauser. The poor food is matched by the poor seating; the four adults have resolved into the most awkward arrangement possible. When the Bootblack does not think anyone is looking, he whispers to J, sometimes directly into her ear. The word "skin" leaks out of the whisper, as does the word "thigh." It is faintly possible that he is discussing the chicken.

That leaves the Duck and the former Mrs. Tannhauser, who are and may always be on estimable terms, to talk about the world, which is what they do and have always done. They spend ten minutes explaining to each other that the vaunted ability of one particular candidate to pick up momentum and power late in his campaign is something of a ruse, as the previous race in which he demonstrated this power should never have been as close as it was to begin with, and in fact is more an illustration of the candidate's ability to nearly lose an election that he should have won handily. The former Mrs. Tannhauser grasps this with both hands, as she likes to say.

After dinner, the Duck goes out back to smoke a cigarette. He takes work with him to calm him down. It's only for a few minutes but he can make some headway in picking songs for the little ducks to sing the following week. The Duck hears some noise and peers around the side of the house, where he sees J and the Bootblack standing next to her car. They are arguing. The Bootblack strikes the signpost with his bicycle lock. It gives a clang that is similar to the sound of a belt buckle striking a jungle gym bar that is damped by the soft hand of a naked woman who is hanging there while she is being worked over consensually by a man of her acquaintance. The Duck's memory for noises is very precise.

The Bootblack says something that maligns the chicken. Then he says something that maligns J. He says that she is insufferable in most ways and good for only a few things and that, to prove it, he is going to take her car and drive to a hotel and stay there. "I'll return it in the morning before you wake up," he says. "That way I don't have to see you, which means that I don't have to be disappointed in you." J cannot or will not respond to this. The Duck can detect her sadness from where he stands. He wants to run out and do violence to the Bootblack, maybe take the keys and stuff them down his stupid mouth, the mouth that only moments ago was eating his chicken and propositioning his friend under his roof. But the Duck is a reasonable man and surmises that the Bootblack would just bring the keys up, one by one.

Back in the house, J is chagrined. The former Mrs. Tannhauser gives her special attention in the interest of healing her. Clearly, there is a wound. The former Mrs. Tannhauser's special attention consists of the kind of diverting small talk that is her forte. "I was reading about the head of Interpol," she says. "A Frenchman named François Zolan. He is a singer and songwriter just like someone else I know."

"Is that so?" J says coldly.

It seems that the former Mrs. Tannhauser may have misread the situation but she presses on. "One of his songs has to do with the work he does. It's a long,

long piece called 'Incident Team.' Wouldn't you think that something like that would compromise security?"

J does not answer.

"What do you think, Gifford?"

The Duck is not present in the conversation though he is present in the room. He is thinking about the little ducks and about the vocal arrangements for one of his favorite recent compositions, which is called "Born Inside the Baker's Head." The first two lines, "Born inside the baker's head / Are many kinds of baker's bread," buoy his heart whenever he hears them. He thinks that the little ducks should do an "oh-ah-ah-oh-ah-ah" after the first line and an "ah-ha-aha" after the second. J's sullenness does not bring him to attention; neither does the former Mrs. Tannhauser's attempts to mitigate that sullenness. What does, finally, is the sound of J storming out without a word.

The Duck follows. He catches up to her outside. She has no car and as a result no way to leave. "I just want to take a walk," she says. "Alone."

"There was a time when we were tied to one another," he says.

"Is that the opening line of one of your stupid songs?"

"No. I am actually talking about a time when we were tied to one another. Remember? With rawhide."

"I can't think about those things now," she says. The implication is that she has other things to think about, and though her tone is hard she is crying underneath: ah-ah-ah-ha-ah-ah.

The Duck has an idea. "Can I interest you in a slow waltz?"

"A what?"

"A slow waltz. A tennis match. A trip to the supermarket." He hopes he does not have to spell out the double entendre.

"I think we have to talk."

"Penny for your thoughts."

"That's not funny."

"Tell me what you want to tell me. That's all I'm saying."

She inhales compositionally. "You know that song you wrote, 'Serving You Lunch Is a Betrayal Given the Fact That I Am Planning on Eating With Somebody Else'?"

"I know it," he says. "I wrote it. I can sing a verse if you want."

"No, no," she says. "I'm describing the situation, not making a request. I'm going to call a cab and head over to the hotel."

"Oh." He steadies himself on the side of the house. "I think I am going to be sick."

"Don't be so dramatic."

But the Duck is not being dramatic. He is being predictive. He is sick. He moves past the former Mrs. Tannhauser in a state of disrepair and retires to his bed. His heart slowly jellies. He dies at half-past ten. He is buried in a fat man's coffin, as he once requested, both because he is somewhat fat and because he superstitiously wants to leave room for a companion, whether J or the former Mrs. Tannhauser or someone he has not yet met. The Duck breaks apart there under the earth, the minerals in him going one way, the water going the other way.

He wakes up at five in the morning, his heart thrumming like a lawn mower engine. The former Mrs. Tannhauser has not stayed over, as she will do now and again, but has left a note telling him to call her when he feels better, or if he does not.

He calls J. "Hello," she says. It is neither question nor statement. The phone is a wall between them.

He strains to hear the Bootblack in the background and he thinks he does: a laugh and a coffee cup clinking awfully. "I am going to stop singing for you," he says to J. He hopes this will break her. "I may even close up *The Duck Knows How to Make the Most of Things*. The little ducks will be out of a job, but who cares?" But he cannot make good on the threat, not even the first part of it, not even for a minute. He sings right then and there, with diminished force but a greater sense of risk. He knows she can hear him over the wall. This is what he has to offer. He hopes it is enough. He does not care if it is enough. It will have to be enough. Enough.

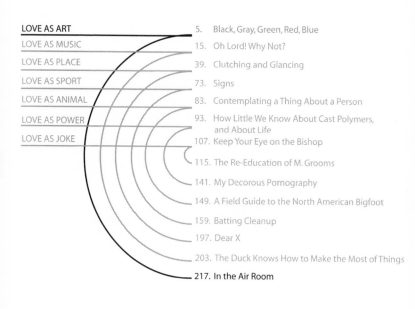

In the Air Room

Boden made the wealthy look good; more to the point, he made them look as they imagined they actually looked. He did not feel as though he was failing as an artist by leaving off with the real. His interest lay in solving problems of light and color he set to himself. He painted Mrs. John Avary, the wife of the university president, standing on a balcony at sunset; the lantern on the table beneath her cast its glow along her neck and jaw line. If he refined her features slightly or returned her figure to what it had been a decade before, what of it? A woman should love the way she looks on a canvas.

The men were no different. When Alex Shawcross, the conductor of the symphony, sat for Boden, he stared straight ahead, as if being interrogated, and in his right hand he clutched a biography of Debussy.

Boden eliminated the book and in its place put spectacles; Shawcross usually wore them but had removed them for the sitting out of vanity. The sleight, which was minor, had major consequences; the canvas, which could have been a portrait of an uneasy man affecting wisdom, showed a wise man at ease.

Boden was only twenty-nine, but he had practiced for years at this kind of improvement. He was a big man with loose skin and one heavy lid, but if you asked those people who had met him what he looked like, they would remember a man of ordinary size and even gaze. It had to do with how he carried himself, deliberate and in a way aloft. He had devised a meditation in which he imagined that all his insecurities—his doubt regarding his talent, his conviction that he was fundamentally unintelligent—filled him and lifted him so that the ground fell away at his feet. What diminished him enlarged him. It was a simple inversion of the truth but it had an irresistible logic to it. He had tried to teach this technique to Shawcross, who he quite liked despite the man's reputation as a martinet, but Shawcross merely crimped his smile and gripped the book tighter.

It was as a result of these paintings that Boden came to Landesman, or rather that Landesman came to Boden. Boden's dealer, an eager young man named Meredith who was always apologizing that he could not do more with an artist of Boden's abilities, told him that a rich businessman had called inquiring after a painting. He did not say how rich, which was just as well. As much as Boden wished to separate what he did and what he was paid to do it—the two had never been unacquainted, utterly, but rather held apart from one another—he had always had a weakness for the numbers. A man's worth swayed him. Boden not only saw clearly that he could be blinded by wealth; he also saw that he could be blinded, as it were, by seeing, and for that reason he refused to meet a prospective client until he had agreed on terms for a portrait. Meredith, as usual, set up a telephone interview with the interested party; Boden stood by and waited for the call.

On the phone, Landesman's voice was a comfortable thing, deep and soft, with more than a little care in it. He was curious about Boden, which was a rarity; no sooner had preliminaries been exchanged than he asked after Boden's accent. "I am a German who just missed being a German," Boden said, as he always said when asked this question. He had lived in the city his whole life, but he also had lived much of that time at home with his mother, who had fled Konstanz when she was not yet twenty. In departing she packed in haste and took, along with the child she carried, more of the German language than she might have otherwise. Boden grew up speaking an English that was not broken but rather overbuilt, with words piled on top of one another and protruding from the smooth plane of American phrases. When he spoke to his mother, who had since moved back to Germany to care for her elderly parents, he heard the misuse of language in each of her sentences, though he could not hear it in his own. She loved him solidly and even sent a little money every month, along with notes that were written in a rush, as if she were fearful of embarrassing him. Boden visited her once a year, though she was sad it could not be more. She was all alone in Germany, as she told all her friends, and oftentimes had no good idea about what to do with herself. When her son came to see her, she could be useful again, and so she she spent much of her time trying to convince him to come. Boden did not tell Landesman all of this, but he told him enough. Then the throttle of the conversation sputtered out and Boden, foundering a bit, moved on to the matter of the commission. At this, Landesman became brusque. A lifetime of negotiations in the boardroom had cast him firm. "You'll come on Saturday," he said, named a time, and hung up.

The grandeur of Landesman's apartment building was best understood not only by the numbers of men who staffed the place but by the caliber of those men, all of whom possessed a superior sense of ceremony and civility. Boden met them in a series of pulses, the outer doorman, the inner doorman, the lobby attendant. Each introduced himself, shook Boden's hand, and made account of the exchange through brief but robust eye contact, so that Boden felt that these were the finest men he had ever met, and he was fine among them. Only the elevator operator was an exception; as Boden rode up in the small, elegant cab, the tiny crabbed figure, who wore a gray cap and had a stem watch stuffed haphazardly into his vest pocket, kept complaining about the weather, and his wife, and arthritis, and the cupidity of certain millionaires. Boden reached Landesman's floor and hopped out quickly, glad to be done with the man. He had expected to be greeted by a butler, or at the very least to be kept waiting, but he had only to ring the bell once and the door opened. A broad-faced, altogether pleasant-looking man stepped out and said, "Hello. I'm George Landesman." Then he turned and was back inside the doorway. Boden stood there for a moment, looking into the apartment. His eye passed over everything but settled on nothing. There was too much to take in. He followed the man out of simple terror.

The place was cavernous. They went down a long hallway, past rooms with antique furniture, rooms with chandeliers, one room with a massive gilt-wood mirror that ran from floor to ceiling, another with a full-grown tree. Boden even thought he saw a Degas out of the corner of his eye: a flash of tulle, a pointed toe. Landesman did not stop in any of these rooms. Instead, he went straight to the end of the hall, where there was a modest den that was not so different from

Boden's own. Landesman sat down on a green brocade chair and Boden noticed what he had not noticed before: Landesman was immensely fat. His coat, as green as the chair, was buttoned over his stomach but barely; the thread mooring the lowest button was being practically put to the test. Boden began figuring the portrait; he could not eliminate the man's girth, no more than he could eliminate his own. It was everything about the man, a perfect summary of his being: he could not move in the chair easily and he could not move out of it. Boden moved to the window to check the light; the view took the park in a single swoop.

"I realized that on the telephone I didn't tell you why I want this portrait," Landesman said. There was a confidence in his tone and also concern, as if he knew he would be marked out forever by the process and wanted to have his say on it while there was still time. Despite that, he had lost none of his pleasant bearing. Much of the credit for his composure went to his face, which was smooth and pink and seemed never to have been whiskered. It lifted him away slightly from his obvious body and all that it implied. If you took time with his face you found yourself thinking of a man who had it all ahead of him still. He did not look young but he looked new.

He told Boden how he had recently divorced and moved back into the city. His things had needed to come with him, or had at any rate not been permitted to remain behind. The one conspicuous exception was a portrait he had sat for years before with his wife and his children. Now, he wanted a portrait of himself. "I may well die this way," Landesman said, "alone. So I want a preview of what it'll look like." He gave a respectable cough. "I had the idea that I'd like you to paint me working. It's what I do, more than any other thing, and I think any admirably honest portrait would show me at it." Boden expected that they would move to another room, but Landesman stayed in the chair. "I do much of my work from here. It's my office. I have meetings, but when I don't have them, it's all decisions and all on the telephone. I've never been big on the desk." He gave a laugh that was sharp, and also soft. "Though I'm big behind it," he said, patting his stomach. "If you can call it big."

They then got quickly to the sketching. Landesman gave sidelong glances, handled the phone one way and then another. Boden was conscious of the fact that he was watching a performance. This struck him, really, as his introduction to things. He tried above all else to have at the man's hands. As cumbersome as the rest of him was, his hands were surprisingly delicate. He was thinking of Sargent's painting of Paul Helleu on the riverbank, the way the hands seemed guided by a separate intelligence to completion of their task. Then he moved up to the head. There was something about it that carried the sketch immensely into authority. What he was seeking in it was the drive of the idea.

After an hour, Boden stood to leave. Landesman cupped a hand over the telephone. "Going?" he said.

"For the day," Boden said. In fact it was for good. He did not want any more. It would be too much. Upon leaving, he could remember little of the afternoon, except for the sense that it had been excellent for him. He stood downstairs, in the lobby, and thought about the man and what he already had come to mean. Usually at this point in the process, Boden had to push himself forward into a painting—eventually he'd get there, but the early stages were filled with negotiation. He had to tell himself, somewhat paternally, that money was not necessarily corrupt, that even an artist needed to survive, and that more to the point it was a form of criticism: those who saw his talent also saw clear to pay for it. With Landesman, Boden had no such ambivalence. He had asked to be painted and Boden, upon visiting his apartment, had felt the strength of it, of both the meeting and the man. Though Boden knew he would paint Landesman in his chair, as he had requested, he could not erase the final image of the afternoon, when Landesman rose and took Boden's hand in his own with a strength that somehow still suggested restraint. There was clearly more in reserve.

Next door to Landesman's apartment building

there was a restaurant, rather deluxe: Boden took a seat at the bar and did what he always did: he read philosophy. He read not to understand, or not only, but to be understood; he hoped that a fragment of the work would, shaken out, illuminate him. He brought a different book with him each time; now, it was Poincaré on mathematics, and Boden, speeding through, felt straightened logically. His head cleared by degrees, and settled, as it always did, on the hope that he would not, after he primed the linen to medium value, washed off his brushes, and mixed his paints, miss the mark entirely. The job, as it were, was to both fix Landesman's character and allow it to range freely over the canvas. And that character, fiercely contemporary, posed a formidable challenge. Boden had read, not in the Poincaré but elsewhere, that in the modern era, subtlety of thought had grown at the expense of stability of soul, and he rose thrillingly to the prospect that Landesman might essentially disprove this notion.

Boden looked around the bar. There were a number of couples trading whispers, a few men, all wonderers and starers, and a handful of women he could make out as unescorted, including a richly blond woman seated down the way. Her beauty was a thing of the past, though not so remotely, but she would not meet his eye, no matter how many times he forced himself down into the Poincaré and looked up in an imitation, he admitted to himself, of contemplation. She withdrew a slim telephone from her handbag, made one call and then another, and it occurred to Boden that she might in fact be waiting for a companion. Presently his suspicion was confirmed with the arrival of a second blond. She kissed the first woman quickly on the cheek, sat down, and ordered a drink for herself, all in one fluid motion that was like the unspooling of a ribbon. She was younger, less done up than the first and even more to look at, especially in her smooth broad brow and her bright level gaze. Boden would have redoubled his effort, for there was every reason to, but before he could close up his book, the two women were upright and away, out into the night.

The next morning, he took it right to the portrait. It was four feet square. They all were. In other cases, he had used the space on either side of the subject to display an array of personal effects, or to paint a window through which a bit of natural beauty might be glimpsed. Landesman, filling his green brocade chair, filled the frame, and Boden put so little space around him, superficially, that his corpulence showed on the canvas in an extraordinary fashion. Landesman did not just suggest reassurance; he was, in short, a demonstration of it. Boden practiced a fleetness and kept the black out for the most part; he needed to keep his conception of the man as light as possible, and he knew that the image should, as it were, rise to the middle of the canvas. Boden worked through the day and cleaned his brushes and stepped back and, looking at the whole of it, felt certain that he had painted a man.

Landesman was delighted by the result. "I said it to Meredith and I'll say it again," he said. Then, after a pause, "Come by Thursday for dinner." Boden assumed it would be a grand party. He didn't have a specific idea of glamour but rather a general one, in which champagne went around on round silver trays and the city's finest, the Avarys and Shawcrosses among them, looked at one another with a mix of approval and contempt. He assumed they would have cocktails in the room with the chandelier and then dine in the room with the gilt-wood mirror. After-dinner drinks in the room with the tree would follow, and maybe he would even see the Degas, if that's what it was. But when he got to the apartment, his only good suit jacket buttoned high to cover a stain on his only good tie, Landesman again came to the door himself, wearing the same green jacket and the same expression of jollity. "Andreas," he said. He was virtually alone in his use of the first name. "Come in. We're having sandwiches."

Boden laughed, but it was true. The two of them went down the hall to the same room as before, where Landesman touched a panel on the wall. It slid to reveal a television set, and the two of them ate roast beef and turkey sandwiches and watched football and talked.

Landesman had many things on his mind; if he had been reticent the first time, he was equally voluble now. He spoke about his daughter, a Seattle schoolteacher who had also recently divorced. He spoke about his son, who, after trying to strike out on his own, had rejoined the family business and was in Europe discussing the purchase of some manufacturing facilities. He spoke about his father, who had been a small-town lawyer. Then, and at the greatest length, he spoke about his grandfather, who had been a barnstormer in the twenties, and then built airplanes for a living. It was the source of the family money. "My father was a wonderful man, but he kept to himself. My grandfather taught me most of what I know," Landesman said. "I look like him: he was thin when he was young, when he flew, but by the time I knew him, he was almost round. He's the one who got me started on planes."

"Started how?"

Landesman turned the sound down on the television. "Oh," he said. "I haven't told you about the Air Room, have I?" As a young man, Landesman began to collect airplane models, books, and magazines about early aviation, and rare letters in the field, and over the years he had assembled one of the largest private collections in the world on early aviation. The papers and objects, which had been housed in the suburbs, had recently arrived at his apartment, and he had hired a man to create special cabinets and shelves for the books and models. "His name is Red Hyde. Top designer for this kind of thing. What we're going for is a world-class library."

"How big is the room?"

"It's big. You could fit three or four of this room inside it. I'd show it to you, but there's nothing to see yet, and lots of exposed wiring and sharp tools scattered around. You can see it the next time, maybe." Boden was surprised to hear that there would be a next time; the information brought him to his feet as if he were being dismissed.

"Wait," Landesman said, pointing to an envelope on an end table. "Take that."

"What is it?"

"It's your payment for the painting. I adjusted it as I saw fit. Generally, I like to pay the price I'm sure I should pay."

"I understand," Boden said, though he could not imagine that he did.

"You look worried," Landesman said. "Don't be. It's higher than you think. But I want to ask you something. I have been thinking about painting, about what it must take." His large pink face had come expressly into its own with regard for his own curiosity. "It occurs to me, the more I let it, that this must be very lonely work." Boden waited for the question, but none came. He folded Landesman's check and turned to leave the room: ten feet separated the two men and then forty, and then he was on the street below, looking up at the high window. He went to the same bar as before, and it was mostly empty, and he populated it with thoughts of his good fortune. Before Landesman, it had been a strange and average year, with many people acting in disappointing fashion, and now and again a reprieve. But then he had met a man who, in a single glance, took him in. When the two men had first met, Boden had not been on the same level as Landesman. How could he have been? But the care with which the older man placed his faith in Boden served as a sort of elevation. He went out to the street, where he stood and looked back up the side of the building. Boden understood the whole thing, or meant to.

What Landesman had said that second afternoon was true enough. There was always in Boden a loneliness so profound that he did not even try to take a measure of its depths. When he made new friends, he put himself through a regimen of interest and gratitude, though he had no thought of maintaining any contact closer than acquaintanceship; when he met a woman, his mind was already moving past her to try to understand the moment when he would be without her. He did not know why he was this way, only that he had never been otherwise. When his mother put him on the train for his first year of university, he had kissed her on the cheek and taken his seat quite secure in the knowledge that he would never see her again. The arrival of a letter from her four days later shocked him. But in placing the strongest light on the darkest of his attributes, Landesman had somehow taken hold of Boden's spirits and lifted them. Boden had not seen the man since he had eaten with him, but he had no doubts that he would see him again, and in fact he could not remember a time when the man had not been vividly present to him.

Boden had also been thinking about the young woman he had seen when he left Landesman's, and that in turn led him to thinking about bars, not the philosophy of them but the fact. It was a simple trigger and a foolish one, but the shot came off, and he started to spend his evenings downtown, with the clear purpose of vodka set before him. As he sat there, the idea came to him that he should paint the scene or, at the minimum, try his hand at something other than portraits. The thought had come to him before: pleased as he was of his work, he could not boast of a following, and he wanted to. In a way, the success of the portraits ensured this particular failure, for each time he delivered a painting, it worked to make a connection with a single subject, and as a result failed to connect with the larger public. But executing another type of painting, particularly a crowd scene, was no small task; if Boden was not paid to do so, he noticed very little about other people. He was practically ignorant of their posture, their gestures, and their expressions. The notion that a large group might come clear to him was distant, at best. But he was determined to stay afloat in this idea, and Landesman's confidence buoyed him.

One night, he took his sketch pad along with him. The hour was not yet late, and the bar not yet crowded, and so he took the corner stool at the bar, set his pad in front of him, next to the slim volume of photographs of portraits that he always carried, in case he ran across a prospective patron, and began to draw. At once he saw into the scene. Though the countertop positively shone, there was a dinginess to the rest of the place: the people seemed tired, at the end of something. He moved along briskly, capturing the bend in a waiter's arm when he set a plate, the bartender at full liberty with both her interest and her scorn. He drew himself out to a great extent, but when he glanced down at the pad, what he saw surprised him. It was a drawing predominantly of one woman, a porcelain brunette about his age who sat as a balance, directly opposite him at the bar, with a lit cigarette moving slowly in her hand, like a considered commentary, and an empty seat beside her. She saw him looking and looked back, ticking her eyebrows upward just a bit. It was the expression of someone waiting her turn.

"What are you drinking?" he said after he had packed up his things and gone across the way. Upon closer inspection, the stool didn't look as if it would bear his weight; instead he stood and leaned.

"I have been drinking rum," she said. "Quite a lot of it, in fact." Her voice was steady, unlike her eyes. She wore a gold shift dress, metallic, with a rhinestone trim around the collar that looked, upon closer inspection, like hundreds of tiny crowns.

"Would you like one more?" he said. "I'll buy."

"Now why would you do something like that?"

"Why wouldn't I?" he said. As a younger man he had a barbaric habit of pouring himself out to everybody, especially women. He would open his mouth and it was as if he had sprung a leak: his history, his dreams, his desires would get away from him, invisibly and immeasurably. But time had made him into a different type. "I have been sketching here at the bar, and you're in at least one sketch. So I figure that you deserve some kind of reward."

"Oh," she said. "And are you a professional at this drawing business?"

"I am."

"What type of artist?"

"Portrait painter by trade."

"That's very old-fashioned," she said. "How did you get into it?"

"I was always interested in drawing and painting, but I had serious difficulty seeing people."

"Seeing that they were there?"

"I mean really seeing them. I got into portraits to bring it all into focus."

He brought out the book of photographs to give her a sense of it, and while he could not bear to show her the Landesman—it was in every way too close—he opened to the Shawcross, which faced on the Avary. "Nice," she said, and went back to her rum.

"And what do you do?" he said.

"These days I drink," she said. "I am an actress by trade." She stubbed out her cigarette and absently reached for another; she had the sense of not wanting to wait her turn.

"Film?"

"No. On the stage. I have done a film here and there, but there's nothing to it. The ones I do don't have the right money in them, and they have too much else. I'm sure you know what I mean." She didn't turn to look at his dishonest nod. "But now that you mention it, it's a film that has me here."

"Oh," he said.

"I was in London for the summer filming and I met a man. An actor." They had been chemists working together for the Allies, in the film, and they fell in love, entirely out of the film. "Up until last month he was doing all right," she said. "Then his letters and calls died right off. So that's what brings me here, all by myself, in the middle of the winter. I have taken up drinking and given up on love."

Boden leaned in farther. His belly bumped against the woman's leg. "Have you ever collected pottery, or vases, or known anyone who has?" he said.

"No."

"Don't you think of love that way when it goes wrong? It's a vase on a shelf that has, after a tremor, fallen and shattered. Would you take all the vases down, or would you leave them on the shelf and bet against a major earthquake?"

"But you assume it's the vases that are shattered," she said, veering a little in tone. "It's not: it's the collector." She spoke so brilliantly that Boden felt certain she was dull.

Boden had come to the bar, of course, to step away from portraiture and inhabit, if only for a moment, a different location within himself. But the more he spoke to the woman, the more he found himself slipping away from that new place. He felt it as a prospect, and so went down the slope, aided by drink, and when he finally did regain his footing he found himself on thoroughly different ground—her knee was beneath his hand, which was re-ascending.

By this time, he had put away the photographs of his portraits, and all that remained of them was a vapor of anecdote, which he navigated through swiftly and cruelly: he lampooned Mrs. Avary's stiff posture and fondness for toy dogs; he imitated Shawcross's gentle lisp; and in short he made sport of his subjects in a manner that was as perfect a betrayal of his true feelings as he could have imagined. He kept off Landesman, but only barely.

"Well," she said, when they had gone the length of the conversation, turned, and come back. "So." The results, as they were, settled in between them.

They took the shortest cut across the remaining business: to the door, to a taxi, to her place. He sketched her in the gold shift and out of it, made short work of himself even before he made it to her bed. What was thickened by the evening hours thinned out in the morning, and he left without waking her, both because she was most beautiful when silent and because he simply had nothing more to say.

The next week, Boden was back at the same bar, taking in the neck, shoulders, and hair of a woman who was in the dining area. She was facing away from him, occasionally checking her watch; her décolletage, he deduced from the slow pace of the waiters passing by her table, must have been remarkable. He knew, the more he looked, who she was: the younger of the two women he had admired the day he had eaten with Landesman. But when he took a step toward her, he knew at once that he had not taken a step toward her. This woman was fainter in figure and in feature; still, the match was high. Boden went back to his spot at the bar. Went back to watch, that is, because she was even more beautiful from afar, especially in the neck and shoulders. Her eyes, too, had something to them; they were green and gray at once. At length, she brightened to something she saw across the room. It was her companion. She gave a faultless wave. Boden followed the line of her devotion and saw Landesman.

He was, as if a point was being made, wearing the same green jacket he had worn in the portrait, and he came powerfully through the dining room and rested a hand on the woman's shoulder. She bent toward him florally and his other hand implicated, if only briefly, her outer thigh. Both of them were brilliant, and it was because of them that Boden left. He departed, in something that was not quite fear, down the street to another bar, trying to make sense of the light rain against his neck. There he sketched what was conclusively a younger crowd, including a woman with a black, strapped dress who spoke continuously in broken French. Then he was outside again, waiting in the mist with his arm outstretched for a taxicab, when a hard jab came at his back. "Give me your wallet," a man's voice said. It was Landesman.

"They meet again," Landesman said. "The painted and the painter."

"What are you doing out?"

"Having a dinner with a young lady," he said. "I just put her into a taxi." He had been drinking, and he brushed off his sleeves with a bit too much industry and then took Boden's arm heavily at the elbow; there was in his grip a connection, positively insistent, to something. "And now I am off to elsewhere. Can I interest you in sharing a cab?"

They stood there on the curb, and though neither man thought to raise his arm to hail a passing taxi, there must have been something about them that was persuasive, for a cab slowed for them. It was not a yellow cab, but a gypsy, and Boden would not have taken it, would not have inflicted it upon Landesman, were it not for the fact that it had a precarious cleanliness, even down to a neatly hand-lettered sign that read, "Leave No Stray Papers Please Thank You." "I'm going uptown," Landesman said. "And then you'll be taking this young gentleman on to wherever he tells you."

They swung out to the highway; Landesman's back was straight. A plane went by overhead. "What's that?" he said. "Looks like a 757 coming out of Kennedy." He was looking away from Boden, and there seemed to be no possibility that he was talking to him. "'The world can never be mastered for more than a few brief moments.' Do you know who said that?" He didn't wait for Boden to answer. "It was Louis Blériot. You must know about Blériot, don't you? First man to cross the English Channel in a plane. He took off at dawn, lost himself at sea in fog, couldn't even tell which way was up. Then he caught sight of the British coast and had to bring himself down quick. Tore up the belly of the thing on landing, but he made it. A few years ago, I bought a painting about that flight: it's a Robert Delaunay from the start of the First World War, *Homage to Blériot*. Do you know it? Very different from your stuff. It's an abstract, mostly." Landesman was flushed now, taken with the progress of his own thoughts. "You know," he said, "Red Hyde came out to start work on the Air Room the other day. Four thousand volumes, all told. Right now they're just a bunch of boxes stacked against the wall. Crates. Tubes with aviation maps. It's going to be magnificent. I'm going to have the shelves covered with black baize so that covers and spines aren't marked up when books are removed. Red also found me a set of floor lamps that look like birds in flight. I even found a company that solves the fire-water problem."

"What's that?" Boden said.

"Books are sensitive creatures. They die by fire but also by water. I have sprinklers that spray halon gas."

Something reached Boden: the man's expansiveness, perhaps. "I didn't know my father," Boden said, wanting to rise to the level of the conversation. "He died a few months before I was born. He was from Friedrichshafen."

"Where?"

"The Graf Zeppelin started around the globe from there."

"Oh." It was the only time that Boden had heard Landesman employ a tone of anything approaching contempt. "I won't have any balloons or zeppelins in the place. No Montgolfier, no Blanchard. This room is for airplanes only." Landesman knew that he had wounded Boden with his unkindness, and he sighed heavily. "You're very talented, as a painter. Even a man like me can see that."

"A man like you?"

"A philistine. A man who makes money and little else. You must look down on a businessman." Boden shook his head. "I never sought this out, you know. Something comes along, a deal is made, and before you know it you have everything." He was still ramrod-straight in his seat. "And you must see what you do. So why do you act as though you have failed?" The spot Landesman had touched was tender, yet the feeling when it was pressed down upon was one of pleasure and not pain. "I don't mean to offend you," Landesman continued, "but I feel safe asking. I think you trust me."

Boden had no reply, or nothing that was not meaningless, and he remained silent. Finally the driver pulled to the side of the road and Landesman left his seat with surprising lightness, walking around to the driver's window to press a large bill into the man's hand. The interior of the cab had been capacious so long as he was there; now that he was gone, Boden felt cramped and he set his head against the window and passed into doubtful rest.

A few days later, Boden was still in bed when the phone jangled in his ear. He lifted it and Meredith's voice came at him through the wire. "I may have something for you," he said.

"What is it?"

"Landesman called. He wants you for a job for his private library. Does that sound familiar to you?"

"The Air Room?"

"Yes. That's it. Can you be there Saturday?"

Boden could, at ten, and he waited at the door for what seemed like an eternity. The elevator operator, who had dropped him off with squinty disregard, fell past the floor from whatever higher floor he had visited, and rose again, all as Boden stood there patiently. It was not like Landesman, and in fact, when the door finally swung open, it was not Landesman. Instead, there was a woman. "Hello," she said. "I'm Sarah. George told me you'd be by." She was directly beautiful, with hair as blond as it was straight, wide emerald eyes, and a face of perfect roundness with pips of healthy pink upon each cheek. "I'm to show you the room." He shook her hand, took in the cut of her green blouse, felt her take him by the knob of his elbow, but it wasn't until she turned and gave him the back of her neck that he recognized her as Landesman's dining companion from the night the two of them had ridden home together. She went down the hall without a doubt, and Boden did his best to follow. Her black leather ankle boots—for that's what Boden had been watching—came to a halt, militarily, one alongside the other, and Sarah leaned into a small white door of half-width that he had taken to be a closet or a bathroom. They were in the Air Room.

It was, as Landesman had said, a library: floor-to-ceiling bookshelves lined all four walls, and there was a large shelf in the center that served as a room divider. But the designer had really done a number on it. Nothing much happened near the ground: a quartet of heavy leather chairs was arranged around small circular tables, and each chair was partnered with an ottoman. The lower shelves, which held oversize books and maps, were constructed as cabinets, with hinged doors that concealed their contents. But in its higher reaches, where the walls gave way to a symphony of arches, the room flourished. Model planes hung by wires in front of framed maps. Instrument panels were set into the mahogany walls. The overhead lamps topping each bookcase offered penniform proof of Landesman's obsession. And, over a fireplace was the Delaunay, a riot of color in circles and, circling them, Blériot's plane, red radiating orange.

"This is it," Sarah said. "Pretty impressive, I think."

"Very," Boden said. "This all came together over

the last few months?"

"Few weeks, really. Do you have any questions?"

Boden took the thing that was closest at hand. "What about this plane?"

"You mean that model right over you? I'm glad you asked. That's a one-sixteenth scale model of a Sopwith 5F1 Dolphin, which was used in combat in World War I. They were powered by a Hispano Suiza two-hundred-horsepower engine, and outfitted with two Vickers machine guns and two Lewis machine guns." She made a quarter-turn, as if winding her presentation, and then continued. "The Dolphins had open cockpits, which model builders like, because they can get more detail that way."

Now Boden began to feel dizzy, as if he were at a great height, and he found his way to the largest of the chairs, a leather throne in rust, and he lowered himself into it. "And what about that one?" he said, indicating a smaller triplane threading a spandrel.

"Oh, that's why I was glad you asked about the Dolphin," Sarah said. "It's the only plane I know anything about, and that's only because I pointed right at it when George asked me the same question." She laughed broadly. "But I sound pretty convincing as an expert, don't I? And here, on your right, you'll see a series of miniatures by the renowned portraitist Andreas Boden."

"Is that what he wants from me? Miniatures?"

"It is." She went to the shelves—they were not lined in baize, but rather painted matte black, like the cabinet doors beneath them—and withdrew a folder from between books. A sheaf of notes came out. "He left instructions, which I'll just read: 'Andreas: Twenty small circular paintings of the earliest pioneers of flight to line upper edge of bookcase in middle of room. See list of names below.' Then the names: Blériot, Chanute, on and on."

"When did he say he'll need them by?"

"He didn't. But he's going to be in Italy for a while, and he said you could have the run of the place until he gets back. He said you did a wonderful portrait of him and he doesn't see why you wouldn't do the same for these people."

"I'm sorry to hear he won't be here. Have you seen the portrait?"

"No. He hasn't shown it to me." She glanced at her watch. "You can stay and look around and sketch. George set aside one book that you can even take with you—it's not a rare volume. Is today a good day to start?"

"It is. Will you be staying here with me?"

A smile exploded on Sarah's face and left behind a faint glow. "Oh, no," she said, glancing at her watch again. "I have to go. I'm meeting a client. Red Hyde will be by in a few hours, and he has keys to lock up afterward. Call me if you need anything else." She clipped a business card to the papers.

When Sarah had gone, Boden settled down with Landesman's notes. Landesman had, on a copy of a photograph, marked the spots where he thought the miniatures should go, ten on each side of the central bookcase, assuming six-inch diameters, although Boden thought he could go even smaller if necessary. Holbein's had been half that size. And while Landesman wanted the paintings to be arranged chronologically, like presidential portraits from Washington on, Boden saw that the effect of them would be wholly improved if they had a sense of chance about them. As for the pioneers themselves, the book that Landesman had set aside for him proved to be both poorly written and incomparably gripping: men were always climbing into contraptions they hardly understood, hurtling briefly skyward, and then crashing back to earth with the full force of their noncomprehension. He got something out of Lilienthal, Chanute, and Ades, and was starting to figure the line on Pilcher, when he fell asleep, thinking as he went that he was experiencing not exactly a loss of altitude from the waking world but the opposite, an ascension to a level that was altogether more empyrean. What woke him was the sound of Red Hyde coming into the room.

Hyde was an inaccuracy. It was not his hide that was red, but rather his hair. Otherwise, he was a stout plug of a man with all the subtlety of a bulldog; when he spoke, it was as if Boden were a small rough patch and he were going over him. "Oh, you're the painter," he said. "Look, if you're going to be in the room, you should know how to be in the room. First of all, the light. The curtains are open now to help dry some of the surfaces, but they really should be kept shut." He glanced at Boden and clucked. "Also, I wish you would sit somewhere other than that chair. I had it built with Mr. Landesman in mind, and I hadn't intended for it to carry a different frame. Maybe the couch for you." He swept his hand wide in summary judgment. "The room has noble proportions; they have to be respected." Boden was coming to his feet and collecting his things, but not quickly enough for Hyde, who reached in his bag and withdrew something in the fashion of a weapon. "I have to take some measurements," Hyde said. "I think it might be easier if I went it alone."

The next day, he called Sarah to ask if he might have keys to the apartment. "I'm not sure that I get along with Hyde," he said.

"How could you?" she said. "He's awful. I'm sorry I inflicted him on you even the once, but I was running late. Can we meet for coffee and I'll give you a set?"

In the coffee shop her eyes were aqua; it was their third color. "How do you know Landesman?" he said.

"Oh," she said. "I was sure he'd said. His son Peter is my husband." She offered no more than this, and

Boden's curiosity held.

"And you're managing the place for him while he's gone?"

"Managing? You can make servitude sound like the best deal going. I watch the place for him, yes. This is an important trip for George. He's in Europe indefinitely. There's something there that's costing him."

"And why isn't your husband helping?"

"He is." Her brow crinkled. "Oh, you mean with the apartment? No, Peter's in business with his father. He's over there helping with the deal. Has been since the fall."

"Have you visited?"

"I went over once. Stayed in the penthouse of a beautiful hotel, ate the finest food, and wanted the whole time to leap out the window."

"You don't like to travel?"

"Oh, it's not the travel. It's what happens—or rather, what doesn't happen—after I get there." She shifted in her seat, and for a second the pattern of light on her face was perfect. "Did you know George before you did his portrait?"

"Oh, no. Not at all. How would I have? But I regret not meeting him earlier."

"Why?"

"I quite like the man. There's something extraordinary about him."

"That there is. To be honest with you, I live in

terror of him—I fear that he will one day treat me fairly." She looked so grave he was certain she was joking. "And then what will become of me? On any particular day I might be given up." She turned to face Boden. "You're lucky so far."

"How do you mean?"

"Beginning as an ally. That's one of his talents, making it safe to be on his side, and in such a way that the menace of the alternative isn't immediately apparent. It comes on slowly like color through water." She saw quite clearly that Boden had balked at "menace." "Well, he is, above all else, a businessman," she said. "When he's challenged, when he's pricked by something, his anger doesn't leak out but rather swells in him. It's a talent. On the other hand, he likes you. There's no mistaking that."

Boden was seized by a sudden fear that if they paused, if they allowed air to be introduced into the conversation, it might rupture the line. "I have a question," he said.

"Of course."

"What's in the other rooms? Apart from the Air Room."

"Everything is in them. He's into everything. He buys what he wants to buy. As he likes to say, that's the condition, if not the definition, of the wealthy. And the wealthy need to feel defined. I have seen plenty of bad weather, but I have never seen anything like the look that comes over him when he doesn't get what he wants."

Boden painted. It was what he did. He set up a small drop cloth on the library table, arranged a line of turpentines, and put down Lawrence Hargrave, Glenn Curtiss, and Samuel Pierpont Langley. Sometimes the going was easy: he loved working out Blériot, who was a smear of mustache topped by lively eyes and a tight leather helmet, and Wilbur Wright with his trademark flat cap. But other subjects eluded him. Octave Chanute, whose goatee and bald pate gave him the look of a community-theater player appearing as Prospero—or worse, "Shakespeare" himself, arrived onstage for a second epilogue—was nothing to Boden, and he could not make headway with the vaguely dashing Henri Farman. Stuck for days on Grahame-White, working only from a tiny photograph in the seam of the *Encyclopedia of Flight*, he cheated with a surreptitious sketch of Red Hyde, who had come to check the levels on the side tables. One afternoon, he wrote to Landesman to ask if he might be permitted to add in a portrait of Bessie Coleman, who had proven irresistible as a figure ever since he had seen a photograph of her in a tight cap that made her look like a nut in its shell. Landesman agreed: "Excellent idea," he e-mailed in reply. "Also Harriet Quimby."

The next day, Landesman sent a message to Boden. "Hyde has written to ask my advice on the uppermost bookshelves," he wrote. "He wants to do them in blue. I think it is better, in a way, to work against that: there is already a 'vault of heaven' with the arches and the light, and I think black is a nicer touch. I have told him this, on the phone and in writing, but I would appreciate it if you would say so, too." Boden promised he would, and he did, though Hyde simply sniffed and looked disparagingly at Boden's shoes.

As the number of miniatures mounted, Boden had a sense that the room might be best served by adding, under the Delaunay, an international assembly of early pilots, arranged to look like the set of zoned clocks in an airport. Landesman rapidly agreed to the cost of the setting and the frame. "For the American I say Beachey," he wrote. "Not a major figure, but one of the most fascinating minor fliers." Boden replied with the utmost brevity, "Russian: Sikorsky?" but he was hardly able to contain his delight with the correspondence. It kept Landesman present, for starters. Though the man was all around him, in a sense, his removal to Europe had wounded Boden somewhat. On days when he knew Hyde would not be in the apartment, Boden sat in the big leather chair and made the most of it.

He quickly developed a fondness for Sarah. It was not simply the presence of Landesman in her, but the absence of anything that was not somehow of him. On her own, she was fine enough to talk to, even more wonderful to see, and she seemed to take to him as well; she liked to marvel at his skill and the modesty with which he wielded it. And yet Boden was forced to admit that there was something about her that was frankly impossible, unknowable rather than simply unknown, without the additional information that she was, chiefly, Landesman's. Before he met her, he had thought of her as an extension of his grand patron, and even after he had met her, as he could glance after her as she left one of their meetings and admire her a posteriori, as it were, he still felt as though he had not known her in even the narrowest sense apart from this fact. Still he was deeply with the girl. What remained fresh to him was, if not his impulse, at least the reasons for it. And so, in short order, the two of them became, in the only way they could, a pair.

He was not capable of much with her, really, for the betrayal would have been absolute, but he liked the moments when he glanced down and saw her red wine, half gone, alongside his nearly empty gin. The two of them also attached others to the course of their evenings. One night, for example, they met a woman who was also a painter; Boden remembered her from a party in the distant past. Sarah had expanded beyond her normal bound and spoke grandly about what Boden was doing. What put the point to him was her flattery: she made the miniatures sound as if they were as ambitious as a cathedral ceiling. The three of them ended up taking a cab back to Landesman's apartment, and Sarah led their new acquaintance through a ten-minute tour; more than a bit tipsy, the woman made a show of her own obedience, counting down the last thirty seconds of her visitation and then leaping out of the room as time expired. The following week, they repeated the exercise with a young magazine writer, who mused aloud at the ostentation of it all and then, optimistically, gave both Sarah and Boden his business card. Boden took to these viewings with a vitality that surprised him. The third sojourn brought back a lordly, graying gallery owner and his new girlfriend, an astonishing redhead who had just graduated college. Boden found both his spirits and his courage aloft, and he even managed to embrace the young woman in the hallway while the gallery owner, inside the Air Room with Sarah, held forth on insectiform flying machines in Bosch. After the couple gathered up their things and departed, Boden, elated, gave gratitude to Sarah, though silently he thanked Landesman; he had not often been social, but, more so, he had not often had anything he wanted to show to others. The room was restoring him.

One evening, at the end of a particularly productive week in which Boden had finally cracked Farman and added Edward Huffaker—a Tennessee glider pilot who came credentialed to Kitty Hawk and was cashiered by the Wrights as a result of poor personal hygiene—Sarah announced over drinks that she was going away for a little while. He assumed it was to visit her husband, if not Landesman, and he began to adjust his sympathies accordingly, but it turned out that she was off to see her mother in California. "She's having a little surgery," she said. "Nothing serious but I'd rather be there." She grasped at his hand; her touch did not linger but he did not withdraw. The next day, Hyde came by early, while Boden was still cleaning his brushes, and after looking askance at Boden's work— he had never said a kind word about it—boasted that he had been hired to design furnishings for a new luxury hotel in Las Vegas, and would be leaving in the morning on the developer's private jet. Boden took a deep breath, filling himself with restraint but also with possibility. With both Hyde and Sarah gone, he could, at last, appropriately repay Landesman.

The next morning he was up early and in the leather throne in the Air Room by nine. For lunch, he took a sandwich into the television room where he had sat with Landesman and ate it ceremoniously. Then, his heart leaping up, he returned to the Air Room, dipped a tiny brush in white paint, and, beautifully, represented on the front of one of the hinged bookcase doors a scene of Otto Lilienthal, in 1894, standing atop a rise in the earth, a glider wing strapped to either arm. The next day he used the same reverse-scrimshaw technique to apply to the adjoining door a tableau of Sir Hiram Maxim's enormous biplane, held down by double rails and powered by steam engine, hurtling forward in its ill-fated maiden voyage. Later that week, he added a clutch of scenes: Charles Manly attempting to lift off in Langley's mammoth aerodrome; Alberto Santos-Dumont perching atop his box-kite aircraft, forward rudder protruding like an oversize proboscis; and Henri Fabre successfully essaying a tail-first takeoff from water. Having filled all available door space on one set of cabinets, he went on to the next. The scenes brought the entire room up, a sense that Boden confirmed by inviting back the gallery owner and his girlfriend, who was, this time, even more enthusiastic about the room if, sadly, no more amorous outside it. The fact that he had not yet, as such, contacted Landesman about the additions struck him as an errant note, out of keeping with the larger harmony, and so he ignored it.

One day, in an otherwise uneventful e-mail, Landesman reported an ankle injury that he had suffered while stepping from a yacht; Boden expressed his condolences. But evidently Landesman's intent was not to communicate the injury so much as to check on the progress of the room. "Is it safe," he wrote, "to assume that the miniatures are all painted and in place?" Boden was high enough in his thoughts of the room that he replied with a puckish tone that he knew at once represented an error in judgment. "Though you cannot prepare for a surprise, you should," he wrote, and Landesman's single-word response, "Surprise?" provoked a longer explanation, somewhat more sober, in which Boden noted that he had executed a few small pen-and-ink drawings of aircraft, including a particularly beautiful Curtiss Model D Headless Pusher, that he thought might be well suited for bookplates. Bookplates: what could be more innocuous? They expressed ownership and pride. Still, the very notion seemed to send Landesman into a state and he took up a rumor he had heard from Red Hyde concerning Boden's habit of showing the Air Room to visitors: it was not the visitors as such that rankled him, but the fact that he had learned from one of them that the room had changed almost entirely. "I am not sure what Red Hyde has heard," Boden wrote back, "but the room is only itself, and that's the best thing you can say for a room. It will please you as it has pleased whoever has seen it." He added, after some deliberation, "I do need another five thousand."

Then came a pause that lasted a few days only but seemed like weeks—the rapid passage of messages to and from had a way of overtaking the clock. Boden waited and worried. He had some other visitors over who agreed with him that the room was coming along like no other room ever had. He checked the mail again and again, finding nothing, and finally, when he was nearly beaten down by silence, saw a message from

Landesman pop up in his inbox. It was a single line
without greeting or salutation or even the courtesy of
punctuation: "Now another report has come in with
more specific intelligence and I have to say I am concerned." Two days later, an amplification followed, a
quartet of long, impassioned sentences that were
clearly the result of a mood of some sort. Landesman,
in them, flailed. Across the distance and the wire, he
seemed to raise his voice, which Boden would have
thought impossible. He could only ignore the tone and
note in reply that four business days had elapsed with
no sign of additional funds.

Landesman's next message arrived so quickly that
Boden wondered if it had already been written: "I do
not know precisely what you wish me to pay for," he
wrote. "Is it these large aviation scenes that I have
heard so much about? All I can say on that score is that
I did not request them and I do not think you should
have involved me in such a large expenditure without
previously telling me of it. Do not live in such rare air."

"Do not live in such rare air." That Boden understood as an irony. But what of living in an agreement?
He directed this question to Landesman, who had his
company draw up a check for $18,200. "I consider that
this will complete our agreement," he wrote.

Boden staged a light protest of a few paragraphs,
but it seemed that Landesman was done with him, or
at the very least, done answering, and so Boden went

harder. He stayed up one night drafting and redrafting a defense of his room, and the message that he sent out in the morning had the feel of a manifesto about it. "You must," he wrote, "see the room and judge it for yourself, and then you will know for certain that your investment is not only justified but a considerable bargain given the wonderful work you have received, which will be something to treasure in perpetuity. You are wrong to treat me as someone who is not presenting you with a gift that would be the envy of any man living. It has been done with the utmost respect and even a tenderness. I should point out that I have not cashed the check for $18,200. As for that payment, I have just noticed a certain slight: on earlier checks, you noted them as payments for 'artwork.' On this, you have written, 'service rendered.' I point this out without comment."

When this letter, too, was ignored, Boden made one last attempt at repair. "I was looking at the shelves and think that maybe you are right. Maybe the entire room should be returned to what it was. It would take black paint only. If this has been ridiculous folly, I apologize. I am optimistic that we will once again breathe the air of friendship."

This did manage to inspire a reply, but Landesman pulled himself up only to push Boden back down again. He had, it seemed, spoken to Sarah, and she had defended Boden, though she had confessed that she had not seen the room in its present state. Landesman was "as appalled as disappointed" that Boden had chosen to enlist Sarah in his defense, and he felt certain that another part of the agreement had been violated. "At this point I do not know what we have between us any longer," he wrote. "I see that you have cashed the check at last. I feel that is wise."

Until the correspondence stiffened, Boden had been generally in a condition of assurance, and, he told himself, not wrong for it. At first Landesman had brought a wonderful accusation against him, that of arrogance, and Boden could not rouse himself to fight it with too much passion. But then Landesman had shifted the indictment toward fraudulence, and that changed Boden's plan if not his mind. Whereas he had become accustomed to spending his mornings walking around the city, the early exchanges with Landesman put him in the Air Room for long days, where he sat quietly. Boden began to see the room as a site of dire exposure, to live in fear that he would return to the apartment to find Hyde there, importantly supervising a crew in the replacing of cabinets and the repainting of doors. Boden fed on his regret. He wrote Landesman a message that he did not send: it was an e-mail, but he wanted an old-fashioned letter, capable of truly drawing blood, and so he printed it out and read it to himself. "I said that we were bound by honor, but now I see that you have none. Hiding behind skirts, or the elevator operator's intelligence, these are both acts of rather comical cowardice. It is loathsome for me to look at this wonderful room now. It is a beautiful achievement, one that towers over anything else I—indeed, many men—have ever achieved. The man who owns this room will be a kind of prince, but I see now that it has been made for the benefit of an ingrate. Once you said that you worried that I considered you a philistine. I did not. Now I see how wrong I was. You are that, and worse." He had no real thought of sending it, but he liked to imagine Landesman deflating with each piercing word. He read it over and over again, sitting in Landesman's large chair. Newly awakened to the notion that Landesman was a man of precarious character—that, perhaps, both of them were—Boden gripped both armrests at once and wondered at how the turn had come.

Sarah, who had returned from California, had been careful at first, and Boden careful in return. But as the week put out its long knives he decided to call.

"Well, hello," Sarah said. "Very nice to hear from you. Have you been busy?"

"I have been," he said.

"And do you have any time for me?" she said, throwing off the implication that he might not. He could not fix on whether her tone was setting the table of the conversation or clearing it.

"Of course," he said. "Come by."

Boden arranged the miniature portraits in a cluster on top of the main reading-table in the library, leaned the extras against spines in the topmost shelves of the low central bookcase, turned on all the lights in the library and all the lights in the hallway, and was sitting on the bench just inside the front door when he heard the scrape of the elevator opening. He stood and opened the door even before Sarah reached it. "Come in," he said, "and follow me. I'd like to show you something." He went briskly down the hall.

"Oh," she said, her voice brightening at his back; his own shadow was visible to him on either side. "You did something to the room?"

"Top secret," he said. "I can't say until you see it. And even then, I'm not sure that I could say." This bit of sprezzatura was the only deception required of him, and for that he was thankful: his heart was chugging in his chest. He opened the library door with a flourish and waved her through. She went, but not all the way. She stood blocking the doorway, taking it all in: the array of miniatures on the table, the extras atop the central case, the cabinet tableaus. "I never imagined that..." she said, and said no more. Boden had prepared himself to plead an excellent case, but the library was its own best defense. The silence drew out between them, stretched to a thinness that was transparent—he could see her motives through it. Then she spoke again. "Oh," she said, and hung at the end of a long exhale. The room filled, slowly, with her breath.

Boden knew from his own portraits that clothing was often a finer second skin that improved people. Sarah gave that theory the lie. When she undid her boots, the thrill was already in the air. Her hair came down around her ears. She guided him to the couch, dug her knees into the cushion on either side of him, and unbuttoned whatever was buttoned. By the time she was out of her dress, she was opulent, almost too much for him, but he took in what he could.

They were together the next night, and the night after that. Boden did not know exactly what he felt, but he knew that he felt it powerfully. The fourth morning, she reminded him of a bit of news—"George will be here Saturday"—and the effect was to inflame and puncture him all at once.

His hair still wet from the shower, he went over to the Air Room. While Sarah had held his face in her hands, while she had murmured his name, he had become clearer on the absolute necessity of a plan. Now he intended to execute it with the same perfection that he had given to the paintings, to the room, to the portrait of Landesman. He began by gathering up his miniatures in a pouched drop cloth and carrying them out of the library. He hid one beneath a cushion in the TV room. He hid one in a closet between leather shoes. He hid one behind the Degas, which turned out to be every bit the thing. He went until the drop cloth was empty, and then returned to the library and stood looking at the Delaunay. Steadying himself against the fireplace, he slipped a putty knife into one corner of the frame and leaned his bulk into it. When the corner gave way, he felt a freedom that he had not known before. He victimized the other corners in quick succession, turned the stretcher and dug out the tacks with the blade, and then rolled up the canvas, which went into the closet with the shoes, into the arm of a coat he doubted Landesman ever wore.

Boden, fully in it now, lined up the turpentines again and laid out the brushes. He needed, and took, the whole of the tabletop to stretch and pin a new canvas, and delivered to the top right corner a bright red stroke. A bright green stroke went beside it. Each became, with time, a blimp. He painted a city around them and, most important, beneath them, but the scale of the blimps remained the very point of the painting. They dwarfed the buildings below, and people were so small as to be invisible. The first day, the two airships were separated by a narrow gulf: the second day he painted, the space between them disappeared. The nose of one bumped the nose of the other. The colors were spectacular.

The jet roared to life, he was pressed back into his seat,

the city growing fainter beneath him, and then he was in Germany, where his mother served him lunch in her apartment and took him out to dinner at a new restaurant down the street. Though she talked constantly, about her neighbors, and her hair, and the pains in her foot, Boden did not listen to her until he asked her a question: "Can you tell me where Father is buried?"

The following morning, Boden borrowed her car and set out for the cemetery. He prepared himself for tears, but when he got there, he broke into laughter. The name on the headstone was like the punch line to a joke he had never heard: it was colorless to him, distant, would have meant the same backward or upside-down. If this was his father, then he was truly fatherless. Boden got back in the car but could not stop himself from laughing. It was in his lungs. It lifted him.

A few days later, an envelope arrived from Meredith and he tore it open greedily. Inside there was a magazine article about the Air Room. Boden spread it out on his mother's kitchen table. All of his disarrangement had been undone: the miniatures were back in place, the tableaus were untouched. And yet, at the same time, his work was nowhere to be seen: over the fireplace, where the blimp painting had been, hung the Delaunay, a mockery in rectangle. There was a caption under the picture, which he read aloud: "The room, designed by Red Hyde, includes contributions from several local artists." Beneath that, there was another article, with pictures of Landesman and Hyde. Beneath that, there was yet another, with a picture of Landesman, Hyde, and Sarah. They stood in a row, arms around each other.

He had brought to Germany, in the inside pocket of his coat, the last letter he had written to Landesman, the one that he had never mailed. He spread it out on his mother's table and recopied it by hand, changing only a few words here and there. His signature at the end was a tremendous, florid thing, both filled with space and occupying all available space.

He put the letter in an envelope and drove along the edge of a storm to the post office, where he smiled hollowly at the clerk, bought a stamp, affixed it. The postbox just inside the door was locked, and the one out in front overstuffed. But the letter had to go. He shoved it into the slot. It went in, but something else came out: an airmail stamp. He could not say for certain whether or not it had come from his letter, only that it fluttered a short distance and landed on the pavement, where the rain came down upon it and, at length, pressed it down.

A Note on the Type

This book is set in a digitized version of Newcastle, a contemporary typeface designed by the twentieth-century Englishman Albert Yarrow. Yarrow was neither a typographer by training nor one by trade. After university, where he studied religion and philosophy, he returned to Kingston upon Hull to manage the produce department in his family's grocery store, though he confided in a letter to his closest college friend that he was "beginning work on a treatise that [would] revolutionize the understanding of the role of faith in modern life," and that he "fully [expected] to labor on it ceaselessly until the end of [his] life."

Yarrow was correct, at least in the latter regard. At his death, he left behind three thick binders fastened shut with twine. His sister Alice shipped the binders to Oxford without reading them, as per Yarrow's instructions. Once at Oxford, they were sent to the librarian of the divinity school, where, beneath the elaborate fan-vaulted ceilings, they were opened. Those assembled gasped. After a title page, on which Yarrow had written "The Heresy of Explanation" (a phrase that would later be re-coined, which is not to say borrowed, by the Biblical scholar Robert Alter), the balance of the binders consisted of a long love letter written to Rebecca Elleman, a young woman who also worked in the Yarrow family's grocery. On the first page of the first binder, Yarrow recalled the first time he met Elleman, when both were eleven years old, and how she had "a single hair" that "stubbornly resisted" being "brushed away" from her "forehead." He had an equally vivid memory of the next day, and the insect bite that "punctuated" her "left forearm" just "below" her "emphatic" and even "angular" elbow. Not every entry was fixated on the physical particulars; "The Heresy of Explanation" also contained long discourses on Elleman's spiritual beliefs, the quality of her imagination, her generosity with gestures of casual affection, and her aptitude for managing the bakery department.

The binders contained little evidence that Yarrow and Elleman had a sustained relationship, though it was clear that they had a strong friendship that sometimes spilled over into romance. One entry in the second binder spoke of "removing" Elleman's "shirt" and "pants" while "laughing" like "hyenas" in the "stockroom." In the third binder, Yarrow confessed his love but also his reluctance to force the issue. "Call it cowardice, or ethics, or call it a form of protection, that I was unwilling to ask of her something that I feared she might not want. I am sustained by the fact that I tried so hard to do the right thing, and also that there was a right thing to do. Did it hurt me? Every day. But orthopraxy, which looks wonderful on the shelf, can slip and fall if you take it down, and the resulting fumes can overwhelm you."

Oh yes, the font. The text in all three binders was handprinted in a meticulous serif face whose individual characters had the look of struck type. The font was dubbed Newcastle, after Elleman's hometown, though she was never told of the content of the binders. The whole of "The Heresy of Explanation," deemed worthless by Oxford, was returned to Kingston upon Hull, where it was buried with Yarrow. He was twenty-three. Oddly, his headstone was lettered in Braggadocio.

Acknowledgments

Many parts of a book are necessary—cover, say, or pages—but acknowledgements have always struck me as peculiar. It's not that there aren't dozens of people who have contributed to my book in most every way imaginable. I am eternally grateful to the friends who stood by me, to the women who stepped away, to the authors I read for inspiration, to the neighbors who watched my kids while I finished up a story, to the editors, the competitors, the gadflies, the mentors. To my parents and my family, especially. But they know who they are, and if they aren't already aware of their role in the process, seeing their name here, back on page four hundred and ninety or whatever, isn't going to do much to fix that.

After much thought, I have devised a solution. Instead of their names, I'll use a numeral that corresponds to the total number of letters in their name. For example, if I wanted to thank Ang Lee, I'd say, "To 6, for directing *The Hulk*." Or, if I wanted to thank Elín Ebba Gunnarsdóttir, I'd say, "To 21, who taught me the true meaning of *lyfseilsskyldur*." Incidentally, neither Ang Lee nor Elín Ebba Gunnarsdóttir helped much at all. They were always busy with their precious work.

So: To 15, for reading. To 14, for letting me read. To 9, for dialogue. To 13, for running that other project (you know which one) into the ground to make way for this one. To 16, though it's been a while. To 11, titanically, for existing both within the stories and without them. To 12, for Ashenden. To 10, for "My Girl Josephine." To a different 14 and a different 12, of course, and to 8 and 18 and 17 and 19. There is strength in numbers.